THE CARNIVAL KIDNAP CAPER

By Dr. Fitzhugh Dodson
and Paula Reuben

Oak Tree Publications, Inc.
Publishers
La Jolla, California

The Carnival Kidnap Caper Text Copyright © 1979 by Dr. Fitzhugh Dodson and Paula Reuben.

First Edition
Manufactured in the United States of America
For information write to: Oak Tree Publications, Inc.
P.O. Box 1012, La Jolla, CA 92038

Library of Congress Cataloging in Publication Data

Dodson, Fitzhugh, 1923–
    The carnival kidnap caper.

    SUMMARY: In a California town of the future five junior high students, using the projects they made for the annual school carnival, uncover a plot to kidnap the Vice President.
    [1. Kidnapping—Fiction 2. Mystery and detective stories. 3. Science fiction]
I.   Reuben, Paula, 1932–   joint author.
II. Title.
PZ7.D686Car   [Fic]   79-20260

ISBN 0-916392-40-6

THE
CARNIVAL
KIDNAP
CAPER

CONTENTS

1 GETTING IT ALL TOGETHER

$\mathbb{W}$illiam Wisdom, better known as Professor, carefully aimed his magnabeam travelight at the treehouse door. He pushed the go button and beamed himself up to the platform of the sky-blue domed structure.

When he reached the platform, he turned off the travelight and placed his palm against the treehouse door. The sensor recognized his hand print, and the door opened for him. Professor was one of two people who were allowed access to this treehouse. He was the first to arrive.

Professor glanced around to make sure everything was in order. The chemical laboratory, with its beakers and test tubes carefully arranged, was in one corner. The kitchen, with its supersonic oven and refrigerator, was in another.

A wafer-thin circular video screen was suspended from the ceiling in the middle of the room. Beneath it was a round table and five cocoon-shaped chairs. Each chair had a control panel in the right armrest. One wall was lined with floor-to-ceiling shelves crammed with books.

Poindexter was quietly reading by the bookcase.

Poindexter was a robot. He was shaped like a gigantic brain with a TV screen inserted in the front cerebrum. He had two arms and rested on a pair of wheels. Although Poindexter had an extraordinary amount of information programmed into his circuits, he preferred reading murder mysteries to solving problems.

"Hi, Poindexter," Professor said.

Poindexter waved absentmindedly and went on reading.

"Don't worry, I won't bother you," said Professor. He selected a book from the shelves. "I've got my own reading to do."

He settled his lanky frame in one of the chairs. Professor was tall—the tallest kid at Hillcrest Junior High. He brushed his light brown hair out of his eyes and opened his book.

He had scarcely begun reading when a buzzer sounded. Professor touched the proper button on his chair control panel and glanced up at the video screen. He saw a girl with blonde curls and a pink dress.

Professor sighed. He put down his book and went out to the treehouse platform.

"You're too early, Mary Jane," he called down. "TJ isn't here yet."

"I know she's not," said Mary Jane. "She had to stop at her locker to pick up the plans. She told me to come here and you'd show me around."

"All right," said Professor. But he didn't look too happy as he magnabeamed down.

He handed Mary Jane an extra travelight and showed her how to beam herself up.

"That was fun!" she exclaimed as they entered the treehouse. "Except my hair got messed up."

She looked around the treehouse with great curiosity.

"What's that?" she asked, pointing to Poindexter.

"Not *what*, who," corrected Professor. "That's Poindexter."

"Oh," said Mary Jane. "He's so . . . he's so . . ."

2

"Convoluted," said Professor. "He looks just like a human brain—only magnified a hundred times. He's full of memory cells. That's why he's so smart. Come on, I'll introduce you."

"Can he talk?" asked Mary Jane.

"No," answered Professor. "He prints out messages on his TV screen. You'll see what I mean." Professor cleared his throat.

"Poindexter," he began, "I'd like . . ."

"Don't bother me now," Poindexter spelled out. "I have three more pages left of *Murder on the Spaceship to Mars* by Bradbury Ray. But I scan fast."

Mary Jane watched, fascinated, as Poindexter finished the book. It took less than a minute. Then he turned and rolled toward them.

"How does he move?" asked Mary Jane.

"He just decides where he wants to be and cogitates himself over there," Professor told her, turning toward the robot. "This is Mary Jane."

Poindexter put out his hand for Mary Jane to shake. Then he printed out:

"I like your smile.

I like your dress.

I even like you.

But your hair's a mess."

"Oh dear," wailed Mary Jane. "I was afraid of that. Isn't there a mirror here anywhere?"

Professor pointed to one. Mary Jane started to fix her curls. But a reflection in the mirror caught her eye.

"Oh!" she exclaimed, turning around. "Is that a gnome doll hanging there on the wall? Let me see him, please, Professor. I'd like to play with him."

"That's no doll. That's Bartholomew!" Professor replied indignantly. "He's another robot."

"Another one? But he looks so different."

"His appearance is different because he performs different tasks," Professor patiently explained. "Bartholomew takes care

3

of things around here. He cleans. And he cooks. And he makes sure nobody comes around here who isn't supposed to."

"How does he work?" asked Mary Jane.

"I'll activate him for you," said Professor, lifting Bartholomew from his hook and setting him on the floor.

When measured from his toes to the top of his brown pointed hat, Bartholomew was just twenty-four inches tall. He had a round, apple-cheeked face and a full white beard. His red velvet pants were tucked into brown leather boots. The rest of his outfit consisted of a white long-sleeved shirt open at the neck and a red velvet vest.

As soon as Professor activated Bartholomew, a red light started blinking at the top of his hat. Bartholomew ran to a cupboard, took out a feather duster, and flicked it over the entire surface of the room. He hopped up and down like a kangaroo whenever he had to reach any place that was high.

"Did TJ's father build him? Does he have any other clothes? Why is he called Bartholomew? Can he . . ."

"Mary Jane," Professor interrupted, "desist the interrogation. Your inquiries will lead me to a calenture of the cranium."

"In other words?" said Mary Jane.

"In other words," said Professor, "your questions are driving me crazy. You know that, when I am calm, whatever I say is perfectly clear. However, as soon as I get excited, I use big words. I just can't help it."

"It must cause problems," said Mary Jane.

"It does. It does," Professor agreed sadly. "When I want to be understood the most, I am understood the least."

"Isn't there anything you can do about it?" asked Mary Jane.

"Another question!" moaned Professor.

"Please let me ask just one more," Mary Jane begged. "And then I'll stop. Honest."

Professor sighed. "Well, as long as it's just one."

4

"TJ hasn't shown me the plans yet," said Mary Jane. "Has she shown them to you?"

"No. But then, I might not understand them. I'm much better at words than blueprints."

"Well, *I'd* understand them." Mary Jane nodded her head emphatically, her blonde curls flying. "I don't know what TJ is being so mysterious about."

"What do you mean, mysterious?" Professor asked.

"Oh, you know," said Mary Jane. "You remember when we heard we could all enter something in this year's carnival? Well, TJ turned to me and said, 'I've got the perfect idea.' But when I asked what it was, she just smiled and said, 'I'll tell you pretty soon.' It's been *two weeks*, and she still hasn't said anything! And if I'm going to have to help build it . . . well, I just don't know."

"I wouldn't worry," said Professor. "You know that you can build practically anything. And you can do it fast."

"That's true," agreed Mary Jane. "But I'd still like to know what TJ's planning. I hate secrets."

"You'll probably know in a minute," said Professor, as the warning buzzer sounded. "That's TJ now."

TJ burst into the treehouse with a large rolled-up paper under her arm. Her jeans were ripped at the knees, and one of her braids had come undone. Mary Jane sighed. She was tempted to tell TJ that she looked a mess. But instead she asked, "Do you have the plans?"

"I sure do," said TJ, placing the roll of paper on the table. "Let me tell you what it is first. Then I'll show you the blueprint. You've heard of personality tests, haven't you?"

The others nodded.

"Well," continued TJ, "this machine can test, analyze, and describe a person's personality. And what's more, it does it in color."

"What a superlative proposal! A truly impeccable contrivance!" Professor exclaimed.

TJ looked happy. She knew he was pleased because of his choice of words.

"How does it work?" asked Mary Jane.

TJ unrolled the blueprint. She pushed her thick glasses back from the tip of her nose. "The person who's being tested has to be in a relaxed state, like a light hypnotic trance. Then the subject's hands rest on the sensitive scanning device. The electromagnetic impulses from the hands will attract certain colors of paint which will then dribble slowly onto the paper. The hands will vibrate gently, and these vibrations will make the colors move in a pattern. Then the paper will come out here—a psychological portrait of the subject's inner feelings."

"Hmmmm," said Mary Jane slowly, her finger tracing the blueprint. "Yes. Yes, indeed. It's a great idea, TJ. There's just one thing."

"What's that?" TJ asked. "I haven't forgotten anything, have I?"

"Well," said Mary Jane. "You're great at inventing things. And I'm great at building them. And Professor knows all about patents and words and all that sort of stuff. But we need somebody who's good at chemistry. That paint has to be quick-drying and a certain thickness for it to flow just right. I don't know how to do that stuff."

"Neither do I," said Professor. "And we've got to get somebody who knows about hypnosis as well."

"I've thought of that already," said TJ. "I just wanted to check with you two first to see if you liked the general idea. And since you do, we can tell the others about it when they come."

"Who's coming?" asked TJ.

"You know Cookie Cook?" asked TJ.

"I do," said Professor. "I've translated some recipes from French into English for him. He's that short fat guy who lives near the school."

"I know him, too," said Mary Jane. "He's the kid who's

always passing out cookies. His cookies are good, but what does he know about chemistry?"

"Lots," answered TJ. "As much as you know about motors."

Professor said, "He once told me that cooking is like chemistry. You mix together certain ingredients, and you get predictable results. Only he likes cooking better because he gets to eat the results."

"You can tell that just by looking at him," said Mary Jane. "Who else did you ask?"

"Doc Smith," said TJ, turning on the video scanner to see if the other two had entered the yard. "There they are," she said.

TJ, Mary Jane, and Professor went out onto the treehouse platform.

"Hi," TJ called down to the two newcomers. "I'll toss you a magnabeam travelight, and you can beam on up."

"I won't need one, thanks," said Doc. "I'll just climb up this tree here."

TJ knew there was no way that anybody could get up *that* tree. But she figured that Doc was going to have to find out for herself.

Doc twined her arms and legs around the trunk and started to shinny up. But when she was three-quarters of the way, she suddenly slipped right down to the ground.

"Ouch!" she yelled.

Doc got up and tried once more to climb the tree. But just as soon as she got three-quarters of the way up, she slid down as fast as she had before.

"You're pretty good, Doc," TJ called. "But there's no way you're going to get up here. It may look like an ordinary tree, but it's coated with a special stuff that nobody can climb."

"So that's the reason," said Doc. "I'm glad to hear it isn't me."

TJ tossed down two travelights. After Doc and Cookie had

beamed their way up, all five went inside the treehouse.

"Wow!" said Cookie, looking around. "A chemistry laboratory *and* a kitchen. I'm going to like it here."

"Who are those guys?" asked Doc, pointing to Bartholomew and Poindexter.

"They're the robots my Dad built for me to go with the treehouse," said TJ. "I'll show you around, and then we can talk about the carnival project."

Even though Mary Jane had already seen the treehouse, she followed TJ around and asked a lot more questions. After TJ had answered them all, she unrolled the plans.

"I've already explained this to Mary Jane and Professor," TJ said. "Now I'll tell you. But you both have to promise one thing: if you decide not to work on this with us, you won't tell anybody else about it. Promise?"

"Sure," said Doc. "I promise."

"Me, too," said Cookie.

"Okay, then." TJ unrolled the plans once more and explained how the machine they planned to make would analyze and describe a personality in color.

"Fantastic! Simply fantastic," said Cookie, after TJ had finished explaining.

"Can you make the paint for us?" Mary Jane asked him.

"Sure," said Cookie. "It shouldn't be too much trouble to get it right."

"Then do you want to join us in this project?" TJ asked him.

"Absolutely."

"Good," said TJ. "Now, how about you?" she asked Doc.

"Yes," said Doc slowly. "I want to. I want to very much. Except . . ." Doc shivered. Goosebumps stood out on her dark skin.

"What's the matter?" asked Professor.

"I don't know exactly," said Doc. "You see, I've got extrasensory perception—ESP. And right now I've got a funny feeling that something bad is going to happen around this machine."

"What's going to happen?" asked Mary Jane apprehensively.

"I can't tell," said Doc. "I only know that I've got a certain feeling inside me—the kind of feeling that spells trouble."

"The only trouble I can imagine is if we can't get it done on time," TJ said impatiently. "Doc, do you know anything about hypnosis?"

"Oh, yes, I've been researching the subject," said Doc. "Here, I'll show you a little self-hypnosis. When you snap your fingers, I'll come out of it."

Doc took a deep breath, closed her eyes, and flopped to the floor in a little ball.

"Do you think she's hurt?" asked Mary Jane.

"Naw," said Cookie. "I live next door to her, and I've seen her do it millions of times. She can't feel a thing. Look."

He knelt down beside Doc and pinched her arm. Doc didn't move a muscle.

"You can take off her shoes and tickle the bottoms of her feet, and she won't even giggle. I've seen that, too," Cookie continued.

Professor snapped his fingers. Doc opened her eyes, and uncurled from the little ball position. She stretched her arms and legs, and grinned up at the others.

"You looked just like a cat when you were curled up there," said TJ.

"A big black cat. And I can bring trouble to those who cross my path," Doc told them.

"What do you mean?" asked Mary Jane.

"Well," said Doc, "when we moved to this neighborhood, we were the first black family here."

"I remember that," Cookie said. "Some people were pretty mean to you at first."

"Did you ever get beat up?" asked Mary Jane.

9

"I wasn't going to give anybody a chance," said Doc. "I learned karate. I've got a black belt."

"Then you must be an expert in physical fitness," said Professor.

"Pretty much," said Doc. "But during my training, I learned that you need a good mental outlook, too."

"A sound mind in a sound body," said TJ.

"Exactly," said Doc. "That's how I got interested in psychology and how our minds work. I think I'd like to be a doctor someday. But whatever I'm going to be, one thing is sure. Nobody's going to stop me, or else they'll have to remember how unlucky it can be to cross a black cat's path."

"Mere superstition," said Professor loftily. "Furthermore, black cats are not considered unlucky everywhere. In Japan, for example, a black cat placed on the stomach of someone who is ill is supposed to help cure him. And Welsh sailors believed black cats helped forecast the weather. Furthermore . . ."

"No time for lectures now, Professor," TJ interrupted him, then turned to Doc. "You sure know a lot about hypnosis. Do you want to work with us on our machine?"

Doc nodded.

"That's good," said TJ. "Then it's settled. Except for one thing. We need a name for it."

TJ looked straight at Professor.

"Hmmmm," he said.

"Hmmmm," he said again.

He put his hands behind his back and paced back and forth a few times.

"Hmmm," he said a third time.

The others waited impatiently.

Then he stopped pacing, snapped his fingers, and said, "I've got it! How about the *Perfect Portable Personality Painter?*"

"That's it!" said TJ, and everyone agreed with her.

"Okay, gang," TJ told them. "Here's what we'll do. Mary Jane, you work on the mechanical parts. Cookie, you're in charge of the paint. We need nine colors—red, orange, yellow, green, blue, violet, black, white, and brown. And they've got to be washable, in case someone should spill them by mistake."

"No trouble at all," said Cookie.

"Good. Doc, you and Professor work on getting the right audiovisual combination to put someone into a light hypnotic trance," TJ said. "And I'll work on the time schedule and co-ordinate everything. I think we should be able to have some-thing done by two weeks from today. Okay?"

Everybody nodded.

"Any questions?" asked TJ.

"Yes," said Cookie. "Perfect Portable Personality Painter is an awful lot to say whenever we talk about it. Can't we call it something shorter?"

"That's true," TJ said. "It is a mouthful. What do you say, Professor?"

"I guess we could call it the P-4 for short," he told her.

"That's a lot better," said Cookie.

"Any more questions?" asked TJ.

No one had any. So they all left, except for TJ, who sat alone on the treehouse floor with the plans spread in front of her.

The treehouse was in TJ's back yard. Her father, who was a famous engineer, designed and built it before he left for Ju-piter. He built it for TJ, but when he did, he incorporated ex-perimental equipment that he had been inventing. The trave-lights were something her father started working on before he left two years ago. TJ had finished them.

Her father used to let her watch him work in his home laboratory. He was the first one to call her TJ. She was really Tilda Jean, a name her mother had chosen.

"It's after my grandmother's great-great-aunt," her mother had explained. "She came to California in a covered wagon. I like its sound. It's historical."

"Well, I hate it," TJ told her mother. "It sounds yucky."

She always called herself TJ and never told anyone her real name if she could help it. Her mother was the only one who called her Tilda Jean.

TJ missed her father. She had decided long ago that she was going to become a famous inventor just like him. Not only was she extraordinarily bright, but she also had a photographic memory. She could read a page of any book and then repeat word for word exactly what was on that page. She could also remember in photographic detail pages or diagrams she had read three and five years ago.

TJ looked over the plans again carefully.

"Yes," she said to herself, "I think this is as good an idea as any I've had in a long, long time. I can't wait to see it finished."

2   SHARING A SECRET

$\mathbb{F}$irst period Tuesday was always assembly time for Hillcrest Junior High School. TJ waited outside on the steps for the others so they could sit together. She spotted Mary Jane way down the street in her frilly pink dress. Mary Jane almost always wore frilly pink dresses, except when she was taking apart an engine or something like that. Then she wore pink overalls that her mother had made especially for her.

"Cookie's going to be a little late," said Doc, as she and Professor came up. "I told him that we'd go inside and save him a seat."

The four of them went into the auditorium. Hillcrest was the oldest junior high school in the city, the only one built of brick instead of metal. And it was the only one that had windows. TJ liked it that way. Some people wanted to have it torn down or remodeled because it didn't look modern enough. But other people managed to have it preserved as a historical monument, an example of what architecture was like in the 1970's.

Even though every classroom had the latest electronic video gear and could have the program piped in, Mr. Lyle, the principal, still liked to use the auditorium once a week for assemblies. Just as the first-period bell rang, Cookie rushed to his seat.

"Our ultrasound oven is broken, and I had to use our old-fashioned microwave one," Cookie whispered. "That's why I'm late."

He passed a brown bag of cookies to his friends. Even though it was against school rules to eat in the auditorium, his cookies looked and smelled so good that no one could resist eating them.

Mr. Lyle stepped through the blue velvet stage curtains and up to the middle of the stage. He was wearing his special-announcement, match-the-curtain blue velvet suit. A spotlight shone upon him. There was a rumor that Mr. Lyle had wanted to be an actor, but because he could never remember his lines correctly, he became a school principal instead. Whether this was true or not, Mr. Lyle still liked things to be dramatic when he had an important announcement to make.

Mr. Lyle glanced down at his notes. "You all know there will be a carnival this year, as usual. But our guest will be some-one very special. We will have with us . . ." and here he paused to let the suspense build up, "the Vice President of the United States, Helen Blanchard!"

Everybody in the auditorium started cheering. Except Doc. TJ noticed she was shivering.

"What's the matter?" TJ whispered. "Are you sick?"

"No," answered Doc. "I'm getting that strange feeling again. It's about the carnival. It's about the Vice President. I don't know exactly what it is yet."

"When will you know?" TJ asked.

Doc shrugged her shoulders and slumped down in her seat. "I don't know that either," she said.

Up on the stage, Mr. Lyle was smiling and waving his hands. The photographer from the *Times* took Mr. Lyle's picture.

"You'd think *he* was the Vice President," TJ whispered to Professor.

14

"Ssssh," he answered, poking her in the ribs. "We'll talk about it during lunch."

From up on the stage, Mr. Lyle motioned for everyone to be still. He wanted to continue his speech.

"As some of you may know," he said, "the Vice President attended this school many years ago, and we will be honored to welcome her back. Every year, we have booths for the carnival, but this year, in honor of our special guest, we want the displays to be even better than usual. Please see me about your ideas as soon as you can. I will approve those that are to be part of this year's carnival. That's all."

There was more applause. Students were talking excitedly to each other as they filed quickly out of the auditorium.

Mr. Lyle motioned to the photographer to wait. He hurried over to him and asked, "Would you like to take a picture of me in front of my Rolls Royce? I could pretend I was making the announcement from there."

The photographer said no. In the past year, since he bought the car from an antique car dealer, Mr. Lyle and the Rolls had had their picture in the paper seven times.

The Rolls was a beauty, all right. It had once belonged to a famous rock star of the 1970's. It was a 1975 model and was painted bright yellow. Mr. Lyle kept it polished and gleaming. He even had a special nylaplex shelter built for it right in front of the school where he could see it from his office window. It was his proudest possession.

"I'm sure that will be displayed at the carnival," Professor said to TJ, pointing to the Rolls as they left the auditorium.

"I guess so," she replied. "But I don't care about that. I want to display the P-4 at the carnival. I want it more than anything else in the whole world."

She turned to the others. "I've got something to talk about at lunch. It's important."

Although everyone at Hillcrest Junior High School could sit wherever they wanted to at lunch, there were certain tables that some people thought of as their own. TJ, Mary Jane, and

Professor had sat together in the corner near the water fountain for a long time. Now Cookie and Doc joined them. All of them were eager to start talking about Mr. Lyle's announcements and their own plans for their carnival entry—the Perfect Portable Personality Painter.

"I started to work on the formula for the paint last night," Cookie said. "I don't think I'll have any trouble with it."

"I've been thinking about soothing sounds for the hypnotic trance. I've come to the conclusion that sounds like oooooo and ullllll are the best to use," said Professor.

"That's right," said Doc. "And when we make the hypnotic spiral, it should be in blues and greens. Bright colors, like red, yellow, and orange, excite people. Cool colors make them relax. We can get together on that, Professor, and coordinate the sounds and the colors."

"That's great," said TJ. "How about you, Mary Jane?"

"I should be able to put the machine together in a week or so," she answered, "but there's just one thing I want to ask. What are we going to put it in? I've got a gray metal box that we can use, but it'll look so icky. We've got to be sure it looks inviting."

"I'll take care of that," said Professor. "Abstract expressionism would be the appropriate style."

"Make it pink," said Mary Jane. "That's my favorite color."

"We all know that," said TJ. "But we've got more important things to consider. You know how Doc's been talking about trouble? Well, maybe her ESP is rubbing off on me. Maybe we should add something to the Portable Personality Portrait Painter."

"Like what?" asked Mary Jane.

"Maybe something that would help find criminals before they do bad things," TJ said. "I'm not sure how we could do it, but I think it should be done."

"What do you think should be done?" a voice behind them asked.

The five of them had been so engrossed in their conversation that they hadn't noticed Sam the Snitch.

Sam the Snitch was the nosiest person in the whole school. And probably the nosiest person in the entire city of Hillcrest as well. He always tried to find out everything that was going on. Then he passed this information on to everyone else, whether they were interested or not. Nobody liked Sam.

Sam always dressed as though he were on his way to Sunday school. A shirt and tie, coat and pants, and shiny patent leather shoes. He was the only student who was allowed to call home if he forgot his lunch. That was because his mother brought a note from his doctor saying that Sam would break out in big red bumps if he didn't eat his mother's cooking.

"What're you talking about?" Sam persisted.

No one answered him.

"Are you going to enter anything in the carnival this year?" Sam asked.

There was no reply.

"I am," said Sam. "Do you want to know what it's going to be? I'll just sit down and tell you."

Sam started to pull up a chair.

TJ couldn't stand it any longer. She leapt to her feet. "We're having a private conversation, Sam, and you're not invited. So beam out, will you?"

"I don't have to," said Sam. "I can sit wherever I want."

TJ made her hand into a fist.

"You better not touch me, TJ," Sam said hurriedly, "I have a note from my doctor that says if I get hurt at school, I can sue the school."

TJ just stood there looking at Sam with her fist clenched.

"You better not, TJ," he repeated. "You know what'll happen to you if you hit me."

"No, I don't. But I'm plenty willing to find out."

Just then the bell rang in the cafeteria. Lunch period would be over in five minutes. Students began to pick up trays and toss papers into the trash cans.

17

"Saved by the bell, Sam," said Professor.

TJ turned to the others. "Let's finish talking in the treehouse after school. At least we have some privacy there."

TJ asked Doc and Cookie to come a few minutes earlier that afternoon. When they got there, TJ handed each of them a magnabeam travelight and programmed their hand prints into the treehouse door so it would open for them.

"My Mom said it's okay for my special friends to come over when I'm not here. But you both have to remember that this is *my* treehouse. And if I ever want to be alone here, you've got to leave."

Doc and Cookie agreed to that.

TJ continued, "And you've got to promise never to bring anybody else up here or show anybody how the travelight works or even tell them about it. Not even your family. Promise?"

"Promise," Doc and Cookie said together.

"Okay then," said TJ. "Professor and Mary Jane know all this stuff already, but I wanted to let you know it,too."

By now Professor and Mary Jane had beamed up to join the others.

"Got any ideas about what to add to the P-4?" asked Mary Jane.

"No," said TJ, "but I'll think of something."

"Maybe we could bring along a dog to smell out criminals," Cookie said.

"That's dumb," said Mary Jane. "What'll we do with a dog the rest of the time? Besides, it might bark and scare the criminals away."

"Whatever we do, we should think of the Perfect Portable Personality Painter as more than a toy. We should work together on it to help mankind," said TJ.

"Why don't we have a secret society?" asked Cookie. "My grandfather had one when he was a kid."

"A secret society? That's for third graders," said Mary Jane.

"I think Cookie's got a super suggestion," said Professor. "It's not necessary to constitute a formal organization in order to combine and perform what TJ proposed."

"You mean, something like a club without officers?" asked Doc.

"Exactly," said Professor.

"Can we have a blood ceremony?" asked Cookie. "My grandfather said they stuck their fingers with a pin and mixed their blood together. We could do that."

"Blood!" shrieked Mary Jane. "It might spill all over my new dress."

"We're just going to prick your finger, not chop your hand off," said TJ.

"Besides, you could put your hand in a plastic bag," said Doc.

"No she can't," Professor said. "It just wouldn't do at all. It's not according to the regular procedures. I think we should prick our fingers, mix our blood, and take an oath."

"I agree," said TJ. "But the oath should be something simple. Not your usual stuff, Professor. We should all be able to understand it."

Professor looked insulted. "Well," he said, "let me think."

He paced up and down a few times and said, "Hmmmm." Then he paced some more and said, "How about this: I promise to use my mind to make the world a better place."

"I like it," said Doc. "It's short and to the point."

The others agreed.

"Here's a pin," said Cookie.

"A pin might give us blood poisoning," Doc protested. "A needle is better." She gave each of them a sterile cotton ball doused with alcohol. "Clean the middle finger of your right hand."

She held the needle over a match for a minute. Then she poured a little alcohol on a cotton ball and wiped the needle.

"Now it's sterilized," she said.

Doc pricked the middle finger of everyone's right hand,

19

cleaning the needle each time. A single drop of blood appeared. They stretched out their arms straight, touched their middle fingers together, and chanted, "I promise to use my mind to make the world a better place."

"Look," whispered Professor. "Our arms form the five points of a star."

"Now we're blood brothers and sisters," said TJ.

"Oh, boy, I can't wait to tell my grandfather," said Cookie.

"Oh no, you don't," warned TJ. "You're sworn to secrecy. Nothing we do or say here gets told to anyone—ever—unless we all agree to it. Now let's all promise that again!"

"I promise," everyone quickly said.

"Good," said TJ. "Keeping ordinary secrets is important. There may even be times that are super secret. Then we'll have to communicate with each other without letting anyone know that we're communicating."

"Like a secret code?" asked Cookie.

"Better than that," said TJ.

She pressed her palm against the middle shelf of the left side of the bookcase. What had looked like a row of books was really a drawer.

"Gee," said Doc. "I never thought that wasn't all a bookcase."

"It is a good disguise, isn't it," said TJ. "That's where I keep my father's files. And this."

She reached in and took out a glass bottle about an inch high. The lid had a small brush attached to it.

"What's that?" asked Mary Jane. "It looks like colorless nail polish."

"This is liquid transmitium X," TJ answered.

"Transmitium!" exclaimed Cookie. "That's one of the world's rarest minerals. But I never knew it was liquid. And what does the X stand for?"

"Experimental," said TJ. "When my father synthesized it, he was able to liquefy it as well."

"Wow!" said Cookie. "That's an incredible invention. What's he going to use it for?"

"Before he left for Jupiter, he got it ready for short-range communications," said TJ.

"How short?" asked Doc.

"About ten feet. If you have liquid transmitium X on your middle fingernail and you press it with your thumb, you can send messages to anyone else with a transmitium-coated nail," said TJ.

"Do you actually mean that our fingernails become transmitters and receivers?" asked Mary Jane.

"That's exactly what I mean," said TJ. "You all know Morse code, don't you?"

"Good," she said, as the others nodded. "That way we won't have to learn anything new and complicated."

She painted the middle fingernails of their left hands with the clear liquid.

"When can we try it out?" asked Doc.

"How long will it last?" asked Mary Jane.

"It dries in a minute and lasts six months," TJ said. "We'll try it out now."

She pressed her middle fingernail hard with her thumb five times.

"I feel a tingling in my coated finger," said Professor.

"That lets you know a message is on its way," said TJ. "As soon as you feel that, rest your thumb on your fingernail to receive. I'll send slowly at first."

She pressed her thumb against her left middle fingernail, pressing heavily for dashes, lightly for dots. Looks of concentration gave way to wide grins as the others received the message she was sending.

"This is the most marvelous invention I've ever heard of," said Cookie.

"It's practically thaumaturgic," said Professor. "Like magic," he explained, after noting their puzzled expressions.

"Now we really are a secret organization," said Doc.

"All we need is a name," said TJ.

A name?

Everyone looked thoughtful. Cookie was the first to speak. "Since there are five of us, we could be the Clever Quintuplets," he said.

"That's no good," said Mary Jane. "We're not even related."

"We just now became blood brothers and sisters," said Cookie.

"That's true," Mary Jane agreed. "But we don't all have the same birthday. So we can't call ourselves quintuplets."

"Yeah, I guess you're right," said Cookie. "We'll have to think of something else."

"How about the Happy Hand?" asked Mary Jane. "You know, a hand has five fingers."

Nobody liked that very well either.

"The Fearsome Fivesome?" asked Doc.

"That's even worse," said Mary Jane.

"The Famous Five?" asked TJ.

"We may be famous someday. But we're not yet," said Doc.

"I've got it," said Professor, who had been slowly pacing up and down the room during their discussion. "How about the Fabulous Five?"

The Fabulous Five!

Everybody liked it.

"Wow!" said Cookie. "Now that we've got a club and a name and a secret way of communicating, we've got everything!"

"Oh, no we don't," TJ reminded him. "We don't have a carnival entry. We've got to get busy on the P-4. We want to test it soon."

3 THE FABULOUS FIVE TEST THE P-4

The Fabulous Five worked very hard. Cookie mixed paints in his garage laboratory. Doc worked on the relaxation system. She designed a spiral pattern which expanded and contracted on the hypnotic viewing lens, appearing three-dimensional. Anyone who looked at this design would also hear soothing sounds through the earphones.

Professor was busy with his research on sound selection. As he and Doc worked on the hypnotic effects, they were careful to coordinate with the machinery that Mary Jane was building.

TJ set up schedules and kept everyone on them.

Three weeks later the Perfect Portable Personality Painter was ready to be assembled.

However, one very important part was missing. A special battery which the Fabulous Five had ordered from the factory had not yet arrived. With it, the P-4 would be completely portable: they could carry it anywhere. But since it had not come, TJ was able to create a temporary power system that Mary Jane could substitute. With it, they could make the P-4 work just as long as they plugged it into an electrical outlet.

After hours of hard work, the P-4 was assembled. It didn't look very impressive—just a gray steel box. Professor hadn't painted the fancy cover yet.

As soon as it was ready for testing, everybody wanted to go first. Finally, they drew cards, and Mary Jane won. She sat down and adjusted the earphones. The others crowded around.

"Stand back," she ordered, "you're making me nervous."

TJ pushed the button marked *on*. They all moved away. They were very anxious to see what was going to happen, but they knew the P-4 wouldn't work unless Mary Jane relaxed.

She peered into the special hypnotic viewing lens. She placed her hands on the sensitive scanning device in front of her. The others watched carefully. They could see her relax. They could hear the machine whir and click.

Thirty seconds later a paper emerged from the side. It was the first painted personality picture in history.

"It's mine," said Mary Jane, as the others crowded around. "I want to see it first."

The paper was full of pink lines. "That's pretty good," said Mary Jane. "At least it recognized my favorite color. But what is the meaning of all these strange lines?"

She looked closer and discovered that the lines formed a very small blueprint—or rather, a pinkprint—of the plans for that very machine. The Fabulous Five agreed that this was a very impressive beginning.

Cookie was the next to try the P-4. After he relaxed, his picture turned out to be one of test tubes with circles coming out of them.

"Hmmmm," asked Professor, studying it carefully, "what could those circles be? Carbon dioxide bubbles? Flying saucers?"

Doc looked at it and said they were probably butter-thin cookies.

"Of course!" said Cookie. "That's *exactly* what they are. I promised my mother I'd bake some for dessert tonight, and I almost forgot."

He patted the machine on its top. "Thanks for reminding me, P-4," he said.

Professor's turn was next. His personality picture showed dictionaries in all different colors.

"Superbly splendiferous." Professor looked pleased. "I shall have it framed and display it in my bedroom."

TJ was next. Although everyone else had been able to relax, she found it impossible.

"The P-4 won't work if you don't relax," Doc told her. "Stop being so fidgety."

"I'm *trying*," TJ said.

"Maybe we can make the hypnotic suggestion a little stronger by turning the power up a little higher," said Mary Jane. "I'm sure it won't hurt it."

She fiddled with some knobs. Soon they saw TJ relax. But instead of clicking and whirring as it did for the others, the machine went wild. It made loud noises. It almost jumped off the table.

"What's happening?" asked Professor.

"I don't know. I'd better turn it off quick," said Mary Jane, turning dials hurriedly.

"I hope it's not ruined," said Cookie. "We've spent so much time getting it ready."

Doc thought a bit. "I'm no mechanic," she said, "but I think I know what the problem is. Cookie, you and TJ change places. And Mary Jane, please reset the controls as they were at first and start the machine again."

They did as they were told.

"Now, Cookie, try the P-4 again," Doc told him. The machine whirred and clicked quietly. It worked just the way it had before, right down to the butter-thin cookies.

"It's all right now," said TJ. "What happened when I tried it?"

Doc explained, "TJ, you're just too much for this machine. You've got such a complicated personality, with so many

25

things going on in your mind, that the machine just can't cope with you."

TJ looked embarrassed. "I guess I'll have to invent a smarter machine."

"Better not," said Professor. "It might be bad news if the machine turns out smarter than its inventor."

"I'm not planning to do it now," said TJ impatiently. "Anyhow, it's Doc's turn."

Doc's personality portrait was a surprise to everyone. It showed a nose and a dagger with a single drop of red blood dripping from its point.

"Is that your hidden personality?" Cookie asked, pretending to be horrified.

Doc looked a little embarrassed. However, she insisted that the picture only went to prove how efficient the P-4 really was. She explained, "I've been thinking about something Cookie said the other day about dogs being able to smell out criminals. I started wondering if there was some way that the P-4 could do the same thing."

"Say! That's an idea," said TJ. "Maybe we could sniff criminals out and then prove they are crooks by their painted personality portraits."

"Do you think you can invent something like that?" Doc asked.

"I'm not sure," said TJ, "but I'm going to give it a lot of thought. We might be able to add something to the P-4 later. But there's no time now. We've got to get this ready to show Mr. Lyle tomorrow right after school. We must get his approval to have it in the carnival."

"Will you be coming, too?" asked Doc.

"She has to," said Professor. "Mr. Lyle said he wanted everybody who was working on a project to show up at its demonstration time."

"That's really too bad," said Mary Jane.

"What are you talking about?" asked Doc. "What's the problem with Mr. Lyle and TJ?"

"You don't know?" asked Cookie. "I guess you hadn't moved here then. When we first started at Hillcrest, one of the kids—they used to call him Gorilla, he was so big—asked TJ what her initials stood for."

"And when she wouldn't tell him," Mary Jane interrupted, "he went around asking and asking until he found out."

"It was Sam the Snitch who told him. I'm sure of that," muttered TJ through clenched teeth.

"Anyhow," continued Professor, "when Gorilla came up to TJ and started calling her by her real name and TJ told him to stop, he wouldn't. So TJ just picked him up and threw him over her shoulder. Unfortunately, she hadn't noticed that Mr. Lyle was behind her."

"So Gorilla landed right on Mr. Lyle," said Mary Jane.

"Mr. Lyle has hated her ever since," said Cookie.

"So, whatever you do tomorrow, TJ, don't do anything to make Mr. Lyle angry. If you do, he might not approve our machine," Professor warned.

"I want to get the P-4 in the carnival more than anything else in the world," said TJ. "I'm not going to do *anything* to ruin its chances."

4 MR. LYLE TESTS THE P-4

The next day the Fabulous Five waited in Mr. Lyle's outer office with the P-4. "I'm not sure I should be here," TJ whispered to Professor.

"We had no choice," he whispered back. "When we go into his office, just scrunch down behind me and try to look as inconspicuous as possible. And whatever you do, don't talk—not even a syllable."

TJ sighed. "All right," she promised.

Mrs. Stern, Mr. Lyle's secretary, told them Mr. Lyle was ready for them. As they entered his office, Mr. Lyle took a paper from the folder on his desk.

"So this is the Perfect Portable Personality Painter?" he asked. "That's a long name."

"We call it the P-4 for short," said Professor.

"A good idea. Well, put it over there," said Mr. Lyle, motioning to a corner of his desk. "You invented this all by yourselves?"

The Fabulous Five nodded in unison.

"Let's see who you are. Wisdom, Matthews, Cook, Smith . . . Foster." Mr. Lyle read. He looked up and scowled at TJ. "Yes, I know you." Then Mr. Lyle turned his attention to the P-4. "You claim this is supposed to analyze people's personalities? It doesn't look very impressive."

Mary Jane explained, "This is only a prototype model. It works exactly like the finished one, except for its battery, which is on special order from the factory. The only difference is that we'll have to plug it in today."

"But it looks so ugly," said Mr. Lyle.

Doc explained that the final model would have a much prettier cover.

Mr. Lyle looked doubtful. "You know the Vice President is coming, and we can't have anything go wrong. Have you tested it thoroughly? Are you sure it's safe?"

"We're sure," said Mary Jane.

"Will it do exactly what it's supposed to do?" Mr. Lyle's voice was anxious.

"You can see for yourself," said Professor. "We'd like you to test it now and approve it for the carnival." He put the Perfect Portable Personality Painter right in front of Mr. Lyle.

Mr. Lyle sat down reluctantly. He put on the earphones. He looked into the hypnotic viewing lens. Mary Jane switched the on button.

Just then there was a terrible noise outside. The lights flickered once and then went out.

"What happened?" asked Mr. Lyle. "It must be this thing. Your machine made the lights go out."

He jumped up from the chair. He forgot to take the earphones off and would have pulled the Perfect Portable Personality Painter to the floor if Professor hadn't grabbed it as it was about to slide off the desk. Just then they heard the sound of sirens wailing outside.

Mrs. Stern came running in.

"Mr. Lyle!" she said excitedly. "Outside! In front! A car just crashed into the utility pole. The fire department is on its way. All the lights in the school have gone out!"

"It didn't get to my Rolls Royce, did it?" asked Mr. Lyle, rushing to the window.

"Oh, thank goodness," he said after he had looked. "My car is safe. And it was that crash which made the electricity go out. I thought for a minute there it was . . . ."

"You thought it was our Perfect Portable Personality Painter," said TJ accusingly.

She had forgotten that she was supposed to keep quiet. Professor nudged her sharply in the ribs, but TJ didn't pay any attention. She kept on talking.

"We really meant it when we said that it was safe. I, TJ Foster, personally guarantee that the Perfect Portable Personality Painter is just that—perfect!"

It was lucky that Mr. Lyle was still looking out the window and didn't notice Professor clamp his hand over TJ's mouth and shove her behind him.

"You said you'd keep still," Professor whispered.

"I forgot," TJ whispered back.

Just then the lights went on again.

"Are you ready now?" asked Mary Jane. "We can go ahead with the test."

It was clear that Mr. Lyle was still not eager to try the Perfect Portable Personality Painter. But he didn't have any excuses left. He sat down as before, put on the earphones, placed his palms on the sensitive scanning device, and peered into the hypnotic viewing lens.

Unfortunately, no one realized that when the power was restored it came on at much more than its normal strength for about twenty-five seconds. This extra jolt of electricity remained in the P-4, and when Mary Jane turned it on, it operated at four times its normal capacity.

Instead of gently relaxing Mr. Lyle, it completely hypnotized him. He sat looking glassy-eyed into the machine. His palms leaned heavily on the sensitive scanning device. The machine first made a click-click-clickety-click noise. Then it

31

made a clackety-clack-clack noise. Then, instead of going *whir,* it went *VROOOM.*

All of a sudden, paint begain oozing out of its sides. Then paint started bubbling onto Mr. Lyle's desk. Paint gurgled all over Mr. Lyle's jacket. Paint gushed right into Mr. Lyle's face.

None of the Fabulous Five acted. They stared, open-mouthed and wide-eyed, as Mr. Lyle became covered with paint.

The Fabulous Five were horrified!

The Fabulous Five were mesmerized!

Finally, TJ had the sense to pull the plug. The machine gave a final glub, blug, glug, and then stopped.

The five of them looked at each other without saying a word. Mary Jane leaned over and tapped Mr. Lyle on the shoulder. He didn't say anything. He just stared straight ahead. Cookie shook his shoulder. He didn't respond.

"Doc," said Mary Jane softly, as she pointed to Mr. Lyle sitting there with his eyes wide open, paint dripping all over his face and clothes, "you're the hypnotism expert."

"I'll try," said Doc, but she didn't sound too sure of herself. "He's in the deepest hypnotic trance I've ever seen."

Doc stood in front of Mr. Lyle and snapped her fingers. Nothing happened. She tried it again. Still nothing happened.

"Mr. Lyle," she said, "can you hear me? If you can, shake your head from side to side."

Mr. Lyle didn't move a muscle.

Doc looked worried. She felt his pulse. "At least he's still alive. I think we better get the school nurse."

The others looked to see TJ's reaction to Doc's suggestion. But TJ didn't seem to be paying any attention. Her arms were folded. She was deep in thought and frowning with concentration. TJ had put her phenomenal memory to work. She snapped her fingers.

"Wait a minute," she shouted. "I remember now. I knew I had read it somewhere. The best way to get a person out of a deep trance-like state is to clash cymbals in front of his nose.

They have to be hit in just the right way to produce the tone of E flat. Does anyone know how to do that?"

No one did.

TJ sighed. "I guess it's up to me then. I'm not *positive* I know how to do it, but I think I can. It's the only thing I know that might work."

"I'll get the cymbals," said Cookie. "They're in the band room."

And he dashed away.

"Doc," said TJ, "try again."

"It's no use," Doc said, snapping the fingers on both hands.

"Let's all try," said Professor.

But even though they made a loud sound, Mr. Lyle sat as motionless as before.

Cookie returned a minute later, out of breath, and handed the cymbals to TJ.

"The only trouble," she said as she took them, "is that if this works, I'm going to be the first person he sees when he comes out of that trance. I don't think Mr. Lyle is going to like that." TJ paused for a moment. "I don't think I'm going to like it either."

TJ tested the cymbals by tapping them with her fingernail until she located precisely the spot where E flat would sound when she clashed them together. Then she lifted her arms and brought them together as hard as she could.

CLANG!!!!!!!!!!!!!!!!!!!!!!!!!!!

The roar was enormous.

Mr. Lyle slowly stood up. He blinked his eyes. He looked at TJ. He looked around the room.

"Where am I?" he asked. "What has happened to my desk?" He looked down at his clothes. "What has happened to me?"

Nobody answered.

He looked at TJ again.

"You're responsible for this?" he asked very softly, rubbing his hand across his forehead. "Your machine did this?"

"Uh, yes, sir, uh, I guess it did," TJ stammered.

"But you guaranteed that it would be all right. 'Perfect,' was the way I believe you described it." His voice was so calm that they began to get worried. By all their reasoning, he should have been shouting.

"It was the electricity," Mary Jane started to explain, but Mr. Lyle just waved his hand impatiently.

"No, no," he said, "I don't want to know why."

"But you see, Mr. Lyle," Mary Jane continued, "when the power went off outside. . . "

"Please, Mary Jane, no explanations," insisted Mr. Lyle.

"What she's trying to say, Mr. Lyle," TJ broke in impatiently, "is that it's not the fault of the P-4, it's the fault of the power failure."

Mr. Lyle's calm disappeared. He got very red in the face. "Fault!" he shouted. "Fault!" He banged his fist on the table. "Fault! You're talking to me about whose fault it is!! LOOK AT THIS MESS! LOOK AT ME! GET THAT THING OUT OF HERE. . . IMMEDIATELY!!!"

"I think we'd better leave," said Doc.

TJ approached the desk where Mr. Lyle was sitting, his head between his hands. "Excuse me, Mr. Lyle," she said, "but should we go ahead and get the P-4 ready for the carnival?"

Mr. Lyle only moaned.

"I didn't hear you, Mr. Lyle," TJ said. "I only wanted to know if we should get the P-4 ready for the carnival?"

Professor quickly picked up the P-4. "Here," he said to TJ, thrusting it into her arms. He took her by the shoulders and marched her to the door. "Don't you ever know when to desist speaking?" he hissed. "You take this right home, TJ. We'll manage things here somehow."

5   NOSE IS BORN

TJ sat on the floor in the treehouse. The P-4 lay in one corner, most of its paint-splattered exterior covered by TJ's sweater. The videophone rang—once, twice, three times. TJ ignored it. It rang again. TJ just sat with her arms crossed, looking into space.

"Tilda! Tilda Jean," her mother's voice came from below. "Tilda Jean, your friends are here."

"Tell them I'm sick," said TJ. "I don't want to see anybody."

"We're not anybody," said Professor as he beamed himself up. "We're your friends."

"That's right," said Doc, who was right behind him, followed closely by Cookie and Mary Jane.

"I don't know why you want to be my friends. I acted so dumb yesterday," TJ said. " I don't want to see anybody ever again."

"We figured that out when you locked the gate to your backyard. You've never done that before," said Mary Jane.

"Is that why you had your mother call the school today and tell Mrs. Stern you were sick?" asked Cookie.

TJ didn't answer.

"You're not upset over what happened yesterday with Mr. Lyle, are you?" asked Doc.

"Of course I am!" shouted TJ. "Aren't you?"

"Not really," said Cookie. "We just used my super spot subtractor and cleaned up everything. The paint was washable, you know. The place looks almost like it did before we did the testing."

"And we apologized to Mr. Lyle," said Mary Jane. "He seemed to feel better once things got back to normal."

TJ's face brightened considerably. "Is he going to let the P-4 into the carnival?"

"We thought we better not say anything at all about the P-4," said Professor.

TJ looked gloomy again. "Well," she said slowly, "maybe it was dumb of me just to sit here feeling bad while you did all the work. It sure is nice of you to come cheer me up."

"Oh, that's not the only reason we came," said Doc. "I got an idea about catching criminals."

"Tell TJ," said Mary Jane.

"You know we said something about sniffing them out? Well, when people are planning a crime, they get nervous. And when they get nervous, they sweat. Now all we've got to do is make a machine that can pick up the smell of sweat, find the people who are sweating, then test them out on the P-4. If they test out as criminals, we've got them."

TJ looked lost in thought for a minute.

"Do you like the idea?" asked Doc.

"Yes. Yes, I do! This may just be our chance to do something for the good of humanity," TJ said. She grabbed a piece of paper and a pencil and started scribbling a plan.

"It doesn't have to be big at all," she said as she showed the sketch to Mary Jane. "I've got some of my dad's old micro-circuits. We can practically build it right now. Let's go."

"Where are we going?" asked Doc.

"Out to the athletic field at school. We're all going to run laps so we can get some sweat," said TJ, holding up a sponge and a plastic bottle.

"Run laps!" exclaimed Mary Jane. "I've got on my next-to-favorite dress, and I'm not going to go out and run laps and get all sweaty!"

"I've got to go home and read an encyclopedia," said Professor.

"And I'm starving," said Cookie. "I'll faint from hunger if I have to exercise."

"No excuses from anybody. We're going to build this . . . this . . . what *is* it we're going to build, Professor?"

"Why NOSE, of course," he said. "*N*egative *O*dor *Se*nsing *E*quipment. That's what we're going to build."

"Of course!" said TJ. "If we're going to build a NOSE, then we better get running. And I mean all of us. Last one to the school has to run an extra lap."

"Hey, that's not fair," Cookie protested. "You guys know I'm not in shape."

"You're in too much shape," said Doc, giving him a poke in the stomach. "That's your problem."

"Quit talking and start running," said TJ, taking the lead.

"I can't stand this any more," said Cookie, puffing hard after the first lap. "I'm going to quit."

"Oh, no, you don't," said Doc, placing her hands on his shoulder blades and pushing. "Exercise is good for you."

By the end of three laps, TJ had collected enough sweat to fill the bottle.

Cookie lay groaning on the ground. "If I don't collapse from hunger, I'm going to expire from overrunning. That extra lap did me in."

Doc looked at him coolly.

"You better get in shape," she said. "I'm going to tell your mother to put you on a diet."

"She won't listen to you," said Cookie. "You know how fat she is herself."

Doc shrugged her shoulders. "Come on, Cookie," she

said. "I'd carry you home if I could lift you."

"We'll meet at the treehouse at eight o'clock Saturday morning to assemble NOSE and take it for its first test run," said TJ.

Saturday dawned bright and sunny. TJ had been in the treehouse since 6:30, impatiently waiting for the others.

She activated Bartholomew, who cleaned up the treehouse so they would have room to work. She tried to start a conversation with Poindexter, but he was reading and ignored all her attempts. Discouraged, TJ flipped on the large video screen, turning from channel to channel, trying in vain to find something that interested her.

She considered watching her father's latest videogram from Jupiter, but she'd already memorized it. She looked through some of his old files. On any other day, those would have kept her occupied for hours. But today she kept glancing at the clock, too restless to concentrate.

Mary Jane arrived first, at 7:15.

"What took you so long?" TJ asked.

"What do you mean? I'm three-quarters of an hour early," Mary Jane replied. "I wasn't even sure you'd be awake."

"Me? I've been up for hours."

"Me, too. I can't wait to start."

"I wish they'd get here soon so that . . . " TJ started to say. But she was interrupted by the warning buzzer.

Doc arrived with Professor.

"Where's Cookie?" TJ asked.

"He said he couldn't think on an empty stomach," Doc replied. "He'll be along after he has breakfast."

"Bartholomew could have fed him something," said TJ.

"I told him that. But he said he was sick of revitrated food. He was in the mood for some old-fashioned cooking. He'll be here soon."

"We can get started before he gets here," said Mary Jane.

Just as TJ and Mary Jane finished arranging the microcircuits, Cookie arrived.

"Just in time for lunch," said TJ sarcastically.

"It's only eight o'clock," Cookie answered, ignoring her tone of voice. "Lunch isn't until noon."

The Fabulous Five settled down to work. At ten o'clock TJ firmly clamped on NOSE's cover. Finished, it was about the size of a cigar box. One person could easily carry it.

"That does it," she said. "Now we're going to try it out. Don't forget: the closer NOSE gets to the smell of sweat, the louder it will click."

"Are we going to take the P-4, too?" Doc asked.

"I don't think so," said TJ. "We still don't have that battery, and we may not have a place to plug it in."

"Besides," said Mary Jane, "we may not even find any criminals. Hillcrest is a peaceful place."

TJ gave her a dirty look. "Don't be so negative, Mary Jane. Let's head toward the shopping center."

On their way, NOSE started clicking as they came close to the school.

"There's a criminal behind there," said TJ. "We've got to spring into action."

"What action?" asked Doc. "We forgot to work out a plan before we left."

"Oh darn, that's right!" said TJ. "Well, here's what we'll do. We'll go up to this guy and ask him if he'll come back with us to take a personality test."

"But suppose he won't come?" asked Mary Jane.

"We'll just give him a karate chop and make him come," said TJ.

"I think you'll find that's against the law," said Doc.

"Yeah, I guess you're right," said TJ. "Maybe we should have brought along the P-4 after all. Then we could have made him take the test by twisting his arm or something."

Doc said patiently, "That still would be against the law."

"We'll think of something," TJ said.

Suddenly NOSE's clicking got louder and louder just as though it were about to explode. The criminals—there must have been a lot of them—were on the school grounds. They were behind the tall shrubs next to the gym.

"We've got to do something quick," TJ said. "There's a whole gang of them. Even if we have to break the law, it's for the good of Hillcrest Junior High and for the good of humanity that we get these criminals. Let's go in and karate chop them all."

"Suppose there are more of them than there are of us?" asked Professor.

"We've got the element of surprise on our side," said Doc.

TJ started the countdown.

"Remember what I taught you during those karate lessons," whispered Doc.

When TJ said, "Now," the Fabulous Five charged through the bushes. Unfortunately, they didn't look too carefully at their opponents before they rushed in.

The Fabulous Five had started karate chopping the basketball team that was practicing on the outdoor court!

"Hey! Hey!! HEY!!!" shouted the coach, running this way and that, and almost swallowing the whistle he was blowing. "What the blazes are you doing to my basketball team? We've got a game this afternoon!"

"Basketball team?" asked TJ, stopping suddenly, her hand poised in mid-air. She looked around at the bodies lying on the ground. "You mean these aren't criminals?"

"*Criminals!* Whatever gave you the idea that they were criminals?" cried the coach.

"Well," said TJ, "we invented NOSE. That's a machine to catch criminals. And it started clicking, so we thought we had found some. We thought we were doing a good deed. Only . . . only . . . I guess we weren't."

"We're awfully sorry," said Mary Jane. "We've made a terrible mistake."

"You sure have," said the coach. "The game's supposed to be this afternoon."

"Oh, they'll be all right by then," said Doc. "This only lasts for an hour, and they'll feel fine as soon as they come to."

"You're sure of that?" asked the coach.

"Absolutely," answered Doc. "It's a special kind of karate."

"Whew, that's good news," said the coach. "You sure took us by surprise."

"I'm afraid the surprise was on us," said Professor. "Indubitably, voluminous research remains."

"In other words?" asked Cookie.

"Back to the drawing board," said Professor, "and fast."

6   TWIST YOUR TONGUE FOR TASTY TONGUE TWISTERS

No one was in a very good mood by the time they got back to the treehouse. It was obvious that their first NOSE trial was not much of a success.

"That was awful," sighed Mary Jane.

"I think I know what happened," said TJ. "It wasn't that the machine was wrong. NOSE did exactly what it was supposed to do—it smelled out sweat. And there was a lot of sweat."

"Right about that," said Professor.

TJ continued, "We're going to have to teach NOSE to be more selective. Just plain sweat isn't enough."

"What else is there about criminals that might be handy to know, Doc?" Professor asked. "You're the expert on that subject."

Doc thought for a minute. "Well, criminals usually carry guns or knives. They're both metal. We should have the Negative Odor Sensing Equipment also smell out metal as well as sweat."

"Wait a minute," said Mary Jane. "Just sweat and metal aren't enough. For instance, we could come up behind a fence with a man digging a hole. Suppose it's a hot day. He's sweating. The shovel is metal. Then we make another mistake."

"I see what you mean," said TJ.

"Yes," Doc agreed. "We do need something else. How about gunpowder?"

That seemed like a good idea and one that would not be too difficult to program into the machine. Cookie was assigned the job of producing a metal and a gunpowder smell so that the NOSE could recognize them.

"We must remember that this is still an experimental model," TJ warned them. "It might take several tries before we get it just right."

"I sure hope we get it right before we make any more mistakes," said Mary Jane. "It was awful what we did to the basketball team."

"Everybody makes mistakes now and then," said TJ.

"That was more than just a mistake," said Professor. "We've got to be extra careful from now on."

"I guess there's nothing else we can do until Cookie incorporates the two new smells," said Mary Jane.

"I'll go home and work on it after I eat," said Cookie. "I'm starving!"

"You're always starving," said Doc. "You ought to carry around some of those meal pills."

"I've tried them, but they don't work. Even though I'm getting a full meal, I still feel hungry because they're gone in one swallow. No, I want something that will last a long time."

"Well, why don't you invent it?" said Mary Jane.

"Maybe I will," said Cookie. "Maybe I will."

"Just make sure it's nutritious. If you don't stop eating junk food . . . " Doc started to say.

"Cut it out, Doc," Cookie interrupted. He'd heard too many lectures from her about his eating habits.

"Cookie," Professor wondered, "could you invent something that would coat your tongue when you first ate it, and then you could suck your tongue whenever you got hungry?"

44

"I guess I could," answered Cookie.

"Excellent!" said Professor. "Then you could call them Tasty Tongue Twisters."

Cookie smiled delightedly. "Tasty Tongue Twisters! I'll make them taste as neat as they sound."

The next day Cookie showed up at lunch with some lollipops. He handed one to everyone.

"Lollipops!" exclaimed Mary Jane. "I don't want any. Only little kids eat lollipops."

"They're not lollipops," Cookie explained. "They're Tasty Tongue Twisters. I made my first batch of them last night."

"You're working on Tasty Tongue Twisters!" TJ exploded. "You're supposed to be working on the right smells for NOSE."

"I'm working on that, too. It's just that I got hungry," Cookie explained.

"Here we are, working for the sake of humanity, and all you can think about is your stomach," TJ shouted.

"I'd think about humanity, too, but I can't think of anything except food when I'm hungry. So you better just calm down and be patient, TJ."

"All right," grumbled TJ. "So you invented Tasty Tongue Twisters. Now what?"

"I want everyone to try them," said Cookie.

"Haven't you tried them yourself?" Doc asked suspiciously.

"Nope, I wanted all of us to be in on this historical moment together," Cookie answered.

"Are you positive they're not poisonous?" asked Professor.

Cookie sighed, "I was afraid that one of you was going to ask me that. That's why I didn't try them out on myself first. I wanted you to see I was so positive they were safe, I'd be tasting mine at the same time. You know I wouldn't poison me."

The others agreed that Cookie made a lot of sense.

"What flavor are they?" TJ started to ask, but one quick lick told her what it was.

45

Lemon!

Everyone else realized it at the same time.

Those Tasty Tongue Twisters were so sour that it was all they could do to keep the tears from coming to their eyes.

"What happened? Why are they so sour?" gasped Professor.

"I guess I didn't put in enough sugar," said Cookie. "Mom was low on sugar, and she gets mad if I use up all her supplies. We have a lemon tree in our back yard, so there was plenty of lemon juice."

"So I noticed," said Professor, whose mouth was so puckered up he could hardly speak.

"How long will the sour taste last?" asked Mary Jane.

"I'm not sure," said Cookie.

"Well, it's pretty dumb of you to use us as your guinea pigs," said TJ crossly.

Doc, who lost her voice when she lost her temper, was hopping around, pointing at her tongue with one hand and waving her other fist in Cookie's direction.

"It's getting worse and worse," said Mary Jane. "Won't anything make this taste go away?"

"I don't know that either," answered Cookie. "I told you this was the first time I'd ever tried this. I suppose water might dilute it."

Everyone dashed to the water fountain. TJ got there first, followed immediately by Doc.

"Hurry up," said Doc. Her temper silences were always very short. "Don't drink it all up." She practically pushed TJ away.

Just then Sam the Snitch came up. "Hi, guys," he said. "What's new?"

"Oh not much, Sam," said TJ. "We're just standing here getting a drink of water."

"How's your thing coming for the carnival? I heard Mr. Lyle wasn't too happy about it. Is he going to let you enter it?" Sam asked.

"Why don't you mind your own business and get out of here?" answered TJ.

"I don't have to. I can stand where I want, TJ, and you can't make me do anything I don't want to."

Sam made a face at TJ, who shook her fist at him.

"Wait a minute," said Professor, "I think I can handle this." He turned to Sam.

"Samuel," he began in his loftiest, most professorial tone of voice, "our endeavor encountered an unfortunate concatenation of extenuating circumstances, culminating in its premature demise—a situation we anticipate is only temporary. We are preparing a diversionary project."

"What's that supposed to mean?" asked Sam. "I'm not a walking dictionary. Give it to me in other words."

"In other words . . . " Professor started to say, but Doc interrupted him.

"In other words, Sam, we're working on something else. Would you like a lollipop?" She turned to Cookie. "You do have another one, don't you?"

Cookie raised his head from the water fountain and fished in his back pocket.

"Here," he said, handing a Tasty Tongue Twister to Sam.

Sam looked at it suspiciously. "How come you guys are being so nice to me?" he asked.

"I guess we're sorry about the way we've treated you in the past," said Doc. "We want to make up for it."

"Are you sure you guys aren't putting me on?" Sam asked.

Mary Jane smiled sweetly at him, "Sam, you know we wouldn't do that to you." She sounded so nice that Sam carefully took a small lick.

"You can't tell that way," said TJ. "You have to take a big lick."

Sam did as he was told. He made a terrible face. "Ugh! You guys have poisoned me!" he gasped. "I'm going to die! I'm going to tell Mr. Lyle."

"Oh, just shut up and get a drink of water," said TJ.

As Sam leaned over the fountain, TJ acted as though she were going to push his head into the water, but Doc stopped her, whispering, "He'll probably accuse you of trying to drown him. We don't want any more trouble than we've got already."

The sour taste stayed with them all afternoon. It took away their appetites for dinner, even Cookie's. And that hadn't happened since he was three years old and had his tonsils out.

The next day the others told him that he should perfect the Tasty Tongue Twisters on his own before trying them out on the others.

"Nothing doing," Cookie told them. "If you plan to eat them, then you've got to taste them. We're blood brothers and sisters, and we're all in this together. Here, try these."

That second batch made their tongues swell up so much they couldn't talk all afternoon.

The third batch turned their tongues green, even though Cookie had used red food coloring. No one could figure out how that happened.

TJ told Cookie to stop working on Tasty Tongue Twisters and get on with the NOSE smells, but Cookie said he was working on both.

On the fourth try, Cookie perfected a flavor that tasted like apple pie.

"Deeeeelicious," was the unanimous appraisal.

In addition to tasting good, the Tasty Tongue Twisters had vitamins and minerals blended in so that even someone who had nothing else to eat all day could still get some nourishment, as Doc had insisted.

Cookie also improved them so that, instead of looking like lollipops, they were shaped like small pills that melted on the tongue in ten seconds and coated it completely. After they melted, the taste would last for four hours for a person who tongue-twisted slowly, or for two hours for a fast tongue twister.

Tasty Tongue Twisters didn't make anyone thirsty.
Tasty Tongue Twisters weren't fattening.
Tasty Tongue Twisters were delicious.
Cookie made ten thousand of them.

"What are we going to do with all of these?" asked Mary Jane.

"Don't worry," said Doc, "I have a hunch they'll come in handy."

"One thing I'm going to do is eat them," said Cookie. "That's why I invented them."

"And now that you're through with Tasty Tongue Twisters, how about working on the gunpowder and metal smells for NOSE?" asked TJ.

"Oh, those?" said Cookie. "I've got that done, too."

"It's about time," said TJ. "I'll add them to NOSE tonight, and we can test it tomorrow."

7 NOSE BLOWS IT

The next day the Fabulous Five took NOSE around to a gun store and pointed it at the door.

No reaction.

"I guess not," said TJ. "We've got guns and gunpowder, but no nervous people."

Then the Fabulous Five walked around with NOSE for two days after school. Not once did it go off.

"This neighborhood is too peaceful," grumbled Doc.

"Besides," said Professor, "most criminal activity commences after sundown."

"My mother would never let me go out walking after dark if she knew I was looking for criminals," said Mary Jane.

"Mine either," said Cookie. "I don't think anybody's would."

"Then we won't walk. We'll ride," said TJ.

"My mother wouldn't let me go out on my bike after dark if she knew I was looking for criminals," said Mary Jane. "She doesn't like me to ride my bike after dark anyhow."

"Would she let you ride in a car or a van?" asked TJ.

"A car or a van?" asked Cookie. "None of us is old enough to drive."

"Who'd want to chauffeur us around?" asked Professor.

"Your brother, that's who," said TJ.

"My brother?" asked the astonished Professor. "My brother Warren?"

"Sure," said TJ. "He's the only brother you've got. And besides, he's got a van."

"Warren would never do it. He thinks we're just a bunch of juveniles," Professor said.

"Why don't you ask him up here tomorrow, and we'll talk about it?" asked TJ.

When Warren came the next day and heard what they were asking, his reaction was exactly what Professor predicted.

"You kids must be nuts," he said flatly. "Why would I want to do a dumb thing like that for a bunch of kids?"

"Because you're Professor's brother," said Cookie. "That almost makes you a blood brother of ours."

Warren only laughed.

"Because we're so nice?" asked Mary Jane, smiling at him very sweetly.

"No way," said Warren.

"You'd be helping humanity by assisting us in testing our newly invented criminal-catching equipment," suggested Professor.

"Aw, you guys just want to go joy-riding. You guys didn't invent any criminal-catching equipment."

"We did, too!" shouted TJ. "You think you're so smart because you're eighteen and have your own van. I ought to karate chop you right now."

TJ made a motion with her right hand. Doc grabbed her just before she could go into action.

"Hold it," said Doc. "Warren will drive us around, and I'm going to give him the best reason of all for doing it."

"Oh, yeah?" asked Warren. "And what's that?"

"Money," Doc told him. "Money! And lots of it!"

"Where'd you guys get any money?" asked Warren.

"Yeah," Cookie wondered, "where did we guys get money?"

Doc gave Cookie a dirty look. Then she turned to Warren. "We have something even better than money." She held out her hand with a Tasty Tongue Twister in it.

"What's this?" Warren asked suspiciously. "You guys planning to poison me and steal my van?"

"No way," said Doc. She broke the Tasty Tongue Twister in half and put one half in her mouth.

"If I were going to poison you, I wouldn't do this, would I? Now you take the other half," she said to Warren.

Warren put what was left of the Tasty Tongue Twister in his mouth. He sucked suspiciously. Then his face lit up.

"Hey, this is pretty good," he said. "It tastes just like apple pie."

"That's right," said Doc. "It's nutritious, and the taste lasts for hours."

"I think that's pretty neat," said Warren. "But what's that got to do with me and my van and money?"

"Simple," said Doc. "Cookie here made up a batch of these, and we're going to sell them."

"Yes," said TJ. "We're going to be so rich that we could even buy our own van if we wanted to. We'd do it, too, except none of us is old enough to drive."

Warren Wisdom thought for a minute. Then he said, "Well, I do need the money, so I guess I'll do it. But you guys have got to pay me plenty."

"Don't worry," said TJ. They told Warren to go outside while they held a hurried consultation.

When he came inside, they said, "We'll pay you a hundred dollars plus gas if you'll help us test NOSE. We'll pay you half before we start and half after we're finished. We probably will want you to help us until the carnival. Is that okay?"

"One hundred and fifty," said Warren.

"Too much!" chorused the Fabulous Five.

They finally compromised on one hundred and twenty-five.

"When do I get the money?" asked Warren.

"Come back in ten days, and we'll pay you then," said TJ.

Those ten days went very quickly.

First the Fabulous Five found a company that sold small glass bottles. They combined all the cash they had and bought nine hundred bottles. Then they filled each one with ten Tasty Tongue Twisters. That left some for them to nibble on now and then.

While they were bottling them, TJ took out her calculator. She figured out how much the materials cost, how much the bottles cost, and how much solar power they used while making the Tasty Tongue Twisters. Then she added all this up, decided how much they wanted to make for profit, divided by nine hundred, and quickly came up with the answer that each bottle of ten Tasty Tongue Twisters should sell for one dollar.

Now that they had the Tasty Tongue Twisters ready, the next question was how to sell them.

"I suppose we could put an ad in the school newspaper," said Mary Jane.

"We could go around and knock on people's doors," suggested Doc.

"There are a lot of people who tasted them and said they'd buy some if they could," said Cookie. "People are always asking me for some."

"We could do all that," said TJ. "But I have a better idea. Time is short, and we've got to sell all nine hundred of them fast."

"We could use 'Twist Your Tongue for Tasty Tongue Twisters' as our advertising slogan," said Professor.

"Excellent!" said TJ. "Suppose we hold a contest. The first person who can say 'Twist Your Tongue for Tasty Tongue Twisters' one hundred times without stumbling will get a free bottle."

The others agreed that this was a good idea. They made

some posters advertising the event and put them up at school. So many people wanted to enter the contest that it took all day Saturday. Only one person was able to say "Twist Your Tongue for Tasty Tongue Twisters" one hundred times without stumbling.

All of the kids who entered the contest were so eager to try them that they usually bought a bottle or two right on the spot. By the end of that Saturday, the Fabulous Five were completely sold out. They had made more than enough money to pay Warren for the use of his van. The Fabulous Five put the rest of the money into a savings account at the bank.

Warren agreed to drive them around to test NOSE after they paid him the money as they promised. "I wouldn't do this if I didn't need the money so bad!" he told them.

"Is this your van?" asked Mary Jane. "It's so ugly. You ought to repaint it or something."

"I'm going to. That's why I need the money," Warren answered.

He went on to explain that this was one of the first solar-powered alternate energy engines ever made and naturally, by now, it was almost an antique. He planned to restore it.

"That's why I don't want to be with you guys if you're going to do anything dangerous. I don't want anything to happen to my van," Warren said.

The Fabulous Five assured him that, even though they were going to go out hunting criminals, his van wouldn't be harmed in any way.

They drove to the other side of town. TJ held NOSE up to one of the windows of the van. Warren drove slowly up one street and down the next for almost an hour. There was no sign of any action. NOSE was quiet as could be. Everyone was getting a little bit bored.

"Are you ready to go home now?" Warren asked.

"Not yet," said TJ. "Drive around for another half hour. Then I guess we'll have to go home if nothing turns up."

As soon as Warren turned the next corner, NOSE started

clicking faintly.

"Keep on going," TJ ordered.

Warren drove very slowly and as close to the curb as he could. NOSE was clicking louder and louder. TJ was getting more and more excited.

"Stop the car," she finally ordered. "I'm going after them."

"Not so fast," said Doc.

"Right," said Professor. "We ought to scout around a bit to make sure it isn't too dangerous."

"I think we should call the police," said Mary Jane.

"Nonsense!" said TJ. "There's criminal activity over the wall there, and I'm going to stop it."

"Remember the basketball team," said Cookie.

"We ought to examine this situation with a large amount of caution," insisted Professor.

"Caution!" TJ sneered. "How can we save the world if we have to be cautious all the time? I'll jump over the wall first. If I need you, I'll whistle. But if you don't hear from me or if I don't come back in ten minutes, you guys go get the police."

TJ jumped from the van and headed toward the wall. The others knew it wouldn't do any good to argue with her once she made up her mind.

However, TJ came right back.

"Here," she said to Professor. "Take my glasses. I almost broke them the last time I got into a fight."

"But how will you see?" he said. "You know you're practically blind without them."

"Don't worry about me. I'll manage somehow," she said. "Tell Warren to move the van up under that streetlight. I'll meet you there when I'm through."

TJ dashed off to the wall.

"Hey, read that!" said Doc. As the van came to the streetlight, its lights shone on a large sign.

"Oh my gosh! We've got to stop her," said Professor. "Come on!"

They jumped from the van and dashed over to where TJ

was just reaching the top of the wall.

"You've got to come down," whispered Doc.

"I know it's dangerous, but don't stop me now. I'm going over. I'm not afraid of danger."

"TJ, get down from there right now!" ordered Professor.

"No way!" TJ answered defiantly.

Professor tried to grab her, but the wall was so high he could hardly reach. He jumped up and clutched at her ankle. TJ lost her balance and fell down on top of him.

"What'd you have to stop me for?" TJ shouted at Professor. "I was just about to go in and get those guys. Why don't you mind your own business?"

"Come over here, TJ," Doc said calmly.

She led TJ over to the sign that she and Professor had noticed.

"I can't read it. I don't have my glasses on," said TJ.

"Then I'll read it for you," Doc said. "It says, 'Shooting Tournament Tonight. Sponsored by the Hillcrest Police Department. Prizes for the Best Marksmanship.' "

"It's just a contest?" TJ asked with surprise. "You mean there are no criminals?"

"That's it, TJ," said Doc. "We've got the guns. We've got the gunpowder. We've got all those nervous contestants sweating. And that's all. Now wouldn't you have looked like a complete fool jumping over and karate chopping the police department right in the middle of their shooting contest?"

"You might even have gotten killed," said Cookie.

"We all might have gotten killed," scolded Doc. "It's bad enough to try to take on the whole basketball team, but it's much worse to take on the whole police department!"

"If you'd have called the police like I told you to, you wouldn't have even had to climb the wall," said Mary Jane.

TJ gave her a dirty look and stomped into the van. She didn't say another word to them the whole way home. But she did mumble something to herself about getting contact lenses so that she could see all of the time.

57

8 MORE THAN A SMILE

The next day Doc cornered TJ before school and told her, "We've got to have a long talk about NOSE."

"That's right," said TJ.

"It's got problems," said Doc. "Like last night—we had the right combination of sweat, metal, and gunpowder. But it wasn't enough. Suppose it happened again, and it was another innocent bunch of people. Those were cops. They weren't crooks."

"No," agreed TJ, "they certainly weren't."

"But, just for the sake of argument, let's say they were crooks," Doc persisted. "Suppose they were, and you jumped in and started karate chopping. You would have been in big trouble. They might have shot you. And if all of us had gone in, they might have shot all of us. We could all be dead this very minute."

"That's very true," agreed TJ, who was surprisingly pleasant. Usually she hated anybody telling her she was wrong, but this time all she said was, "I've thought about it a lot, Doc. Let's talk about it with the others at lunch—if Sam the Snitch doesn't interrupt us."

When the Fabulous Five met at lunch, TJ brought up the matter about needing more control over NOSE. Everyone agreed with her, but nobody knew exactly how to carry it out. At first they talked about programming more smells into NOSE, but no one knew exactly what other smells to add. Cookie suggested attaching a camera, but Doc pointed out that you couldn't tell honest people just by the way they looked.

"What we really need," Mary Jane began.

"Is a way to check out whether NOSE is right or not," interrupted TJ. "We need a listening device to check out our suspicions."

"Right," said Mary Jane. "We've got a NOSE. Now we need some ears."

"That's it!" shouted Professor, jumping up. "EARS! Electronic Auditory Receiving System! That's EARS. You said we needed some ears, and now we've got them."

"Sssshhh! Do you want the whole world to hear?" TJ tried to quiet the others down. "You guys have forgotten one thing. We may have the name, but we're still missing something."

"What?" they all looked puzzled.

"We don't have an invention to go with the name," TJ said. "That's what's missing."

"Is that all?" asked Professor. "That doesn't worry me, TJ. You know we can always conjure up an invention with no effort whatsoever."

And Professor was right. It wasn't long before TJ was able to invent a listening device. It looked like an ice cream cone, only twice as large, and it had earphones attached. That was EARS. EARS was able to pick up sounds within a half-mile radius.

"I think we could have gotten up to two miles," TJ said, "but EARS would have been too large. We would have needed a wagon or something to carry it."

EARS was an immediate success. At first, somebody was always wearing the earphones. The Fabulous Five listened in on everything. They overheard telephone conversations. They eavesdropped on their teachers. They heard what parents were planning to give children for their birthdays. They heard what their classmates were saying about them. It was almost like knowing the future. It should have been fun, but it wasn't. At least, not after the first four or five days.

Then Doc explained. "There's no mystery left. If you had x-ray eyes, it wouldn't be very exciting to get presents."

The others knew exactly what she meant.

TJ said, "We've been using this machine to spy on people. It's not honorable. We're getting to be as bad as Sam the Snitch."

As soon as TJ pointed that out, they all knew they had to make a decision. On the one hand, EARS was too valuable to give up completely. On the other, it wasn't right for them to go on eavesdropping on innocent people.

They talked about it for a long time. Finally, TJ suggested they use EARS only when they were doing good deeds, like catching criminals.

Then Mary Jane came up with a good idea. "It shouldn't be too hard to attach EARS to NOSE," she said. "That way, when NOSE clicks, we can listen in on EARS to make sure we really have a crook."

"Excellent," said Professor. "This will ensure our apprehending only scoundrels."

"And not the junior varsity basketball team," added Mary Jane.

"Or the Hillcrest Police Shooting Tournament," said Cookie.

"I KNOW," snapped TJ.

"I think you're taking this personally," Doc told TJ. "It really wasn't all your fault. We didn't have to listen to you."

"Oh, thanks a lot," said TJ sarcastically.

"Things should be better now that we've got EARS attached to NOSE," Doc went on, ignoring TJ's remark. "It ought to keep us out of trouble."

After they combined the two, TJ substituted a flashing red

light for NOSE's clicking sound. That way they couldn't be heard as they approached.

The Fabulous Five still had to test the newly combined NOSE and EARS. However, Warren Wisdom had found a part-time job and refused to drive them around because he didn't need the money any more. The Fabulous Five walked around with NOSE/EARS, but they still didn't have any luck in the daytime, and they couldn't find anybody else to drive them around at night.

And, worst of all, they still didn't know whether they were going to be able to have a booth in the carnival. Mr. Lyle refused to let them show him the Perfect Portable Portrait Painter again, even though they installed the new battery and even though Professor painted a new cover for it. Mr. Lyle refused to talk to them about the P-4, no matter how often they asked for an appointment.

And the carnival was only ten days away.

"We've got to do something," TJ said.

The Fabulous Five were helping some of their classmates build a booth for the carnival. Even though they weren't sure if they were going to enter or not, they didn't think it was right for them not to help make the carnival as successful as possible.

"One of us has just got to go and talk to Mr. Lyle again," said Doc.

"But who?" asked TJ. "I know it shouldn't be me."

No one argued with that.

"I don't think he wants to see any of us if we're going to talk about the P-4 again," said Mary Jane.

"Let's face it," said Professor. "The P-4 is not going to get into the carnival, no matter what."

"I'm afraid you're right," said TJ. She abruptly turned her back towards the others so they wouldn't notice she was almost in tears. "I guess it's silly," she said, sniffing slightly. "It's just that I wanted to have something in the carnival more than anything else in the world."

"Maybe we could enter NOSE and EARS," said Cookie.

TJ looked intently at the others. Her eyes seem magnified behind her thick lenses. "Do you think Mr. Lyle might say that we could?"

Professor shrugged his shoulders. "I don't know, TJ. You know how he feels about us. I can't be sure that he would even let us show them to him."

"But we've got to try," said TJ. "At least we've got to try."

"Maybe we could ask Poindexter," said Cookie. "He might have some suggestions."

"Let's hope he's not in the middle of reading a murder mystery," said TJ. "He never pays attention to anything until he can solve it. But it's worth a try."

As soon as school was out, the Fabulous Five went over to the treehouse and magnabeamed up. Poindexter was shuffling through a pile of paperback books and was about to pick one up.

"Wait a minute, Poindexter. Please wait before you start that book," TJ said.

Letters flashed on and off Poindexter's screen in a meaningless jumble. He seemed to be grumbling about something.

"It'll just take a minute, Poindexter," Cookie pleaded. "Come on, we need your help."

"All right" were the words neatly typed across Poindexter's screen. "But make it quick."

"How can we get Mr. Lyle to let us enter EARS and NOSE in the carnival?" asked Cookie.

Poindexter's screen blinked three times, then the following words appeared:

Try a smile
For Mr. Lyle.

"A smile!" said TJ. "That's not much help."

"I'm afraid you're right," said Professor. "Maybe we can ask him for an alternate solution."

"Poindexter, we don't think smiling's going to do it," said

Doc. "We've got to do something more intense. You don't know Mr. Lyle. He's as set in his ways as the North Pole icecap."

Poindexter immediately flashed:

Being kind and being nice
Sometimes helps to melt the ice.

Then his screen went dark. He picked up a book and hurried toward his favorite reading spot.

"I wonder what that means," said Cookie. "It doesn't seem to be the answer to the question we asked."

"That Poindexter!" said Mary Jane. "Just when we need him most, he answers in riddles."

"Maybe not," said Professor. "Maybe Poindexter is trying to tell us we should do something to make Mr. Lyle like us more."

"Is that what you think he means?" asked Mary Jane. "In that case, I could tune the engine on his Rolls Royce."

"After what happened before, I think Mr. Lyle would consider it a favor if you didn't get closer than twenty feet to his Rolls Royce," said Doc.

"I could make him some cookies," said Cookie. "I could bring him some before school and then casually mention that I had something important to ask him."

"I think that's more like it," Doc sighed. "Why don't we ask Poindexter if that's what he meant."

But Poindexter only flashed a sign. "I am reading. Please do not disturb."

"He's not much help at all," sighed TJ. "I guess we'll have to go it alone."

9   MR. LYLE LISTENS

The next day, the Fabulous Five started their strategy. As Mr. Lyle drove up to the school, Cookie was waiting for him with a plate of cookies. Remembering Poindexter's advice, Cookie was smiling as hard as he could. Mr. Lyle looked at him suspiciously. Ever since the P-4 incident, he seemed to be very nervous around any of the Fabulous Five.

"Oh, Mrs. Stern," he called to his secretary, who was just passing by. "Would you try one of these?"

"Of course, Mr. Lyle," Mrs. Stern said. She bit into a cookie. "Why, these are just delicious," she said.

"They are?" asked Mr. Lyle.

"My, yes! I'll have a few more, thank you," she said, reaching for the plate.

"Ah, good, Mrs. Stern, you're apparently not poisoned. At least, not yet."

"What do you mean?" she asked. "Who made these cookies?"

Mr. Lyle pointed to Cookie.

"Oh, that's why they're so good. He makes the best cookies in the world. I just love them. And he would *never* poison anybody, would you dear?" She smiled at Cookie.

"Oh, no, Mrs. Stern," Cookie said.

"You know that, Mr. Lyle," said Mrs. Stern.

"Of course I do," said Mr. Lyle. "I was only joking."

"I'm sure you were," said Mrs. Stern, nonetheless sounding doubtful. "However, if you're at all worried, I'll be happy to eat them all." She snatched the plate from Mr. Lyle and marched off towards the school.

Mr. Lyle frowned. "All right," he said to Cookie, "what do you want?"

"I'd like to talk about the carnival."

"Not now," snapped Mr. Lyle. "Not ever."

★★★★★

"He said he wouldn't *ever* talk about the carnival," Cookie told the others later. "I think he's beginning to hate me almost as much as he hates TJ."

"Being nice sure didn't work," said TJ. "I'm beginning to think nothing will."

"That's too bad," said Mary Jane, "especially since there's an empty booth now."

"An empty booth!" exclaimed TJ. "How come?"

"The kid who had it is moving tomorrow. She won't be around for the carnival."

"Mr. Lyle will find somebody else," said Doc.

"I don't think so," said Mary Jane. "The kid whose booth it was said he asked *her* to find somebody else. Nobody could have anything ready in time. That's why she asked me. She'd already asked everybody else."

The Fabulous Five looked at each other.

"Do you suppose . . . ?" TJ whispered, her face lighting up.

"I don't know," said Doc. "Mr. Lyle would have to be pretty desperate."

"We're the only ones," said TJ.

"It all depends on how bad he wants to fill that booth," said Cookie.

"It's partly built already," said Mary Jane. "It will look strange to leave it like that."

"Let's go ask him," said TJ.

"Not yet," said Doc. She looked around to make sure that no one could overhear. "Now then," she said, "here's what I suggest we do first."

★★★★★

Mr. Lyle was so busy reading at his desk that he did not notice the window being pushed open from the outside. Nor did he notice the blue paper airplane until it landed right on his desk.

"What's this?" he wondered. Written boldly on the wings was *Fill the empty booth*. Mr. Lyle glanced toward the window. It was closed now. He went over and looked out. No one was in sight.

"Mrs. Stern." Mr. Lyle went to her desk. "Look at this."

Mrs. Stern stopped typing. "It looks like a paper airplane."

"That's what it is. And look at the message."

"Message?" Mrs. Stern's voice was puzzled.

"Right here." Mr. Lyle pointed to the wings. There was no message now. "That's strange. When it flew in the window it had *Fill the empty booth* written on it."

"Well, there's nothing. there now," said Mrs. Stern. "You've been thinking about the carnival a lot lately. Perhaps you just imagined it."

"No," said Mr. Lyle, "I'm sure I saw it written."

But Mrs. Stern had already started typing again. She wasn't listening to him.

When Mr. Lyle was paying for his lunch in the cafeteria, the cashier handed him a piece of blue paper, folded in thirds.

"This has your name on it," she said.

Mr. Lyle unfolded it. *Fill the empty booth*, it said. But even as he read it, the letters started fading. Mr. Lyle blinked and rubbed his eyes. The paper was completely blank. "Who gave this to you?" he asked the cashier.

"No one," she said. "I never noticed it until you came."

When Mr. Lyle went to get his car after school, the now-familiar blue paper was taped to the nylaplex shelter. The writing faded as soon as he read it. And another one was taped to the front door of his house. He knew before he read it exactly what it was going to say. *Fill the empty booth*. And the words always disappeared before he could show it to anyone.

That night Mr. Lyle slept very badly. He dreamed that it was the day of the carnival. He was showing Vice President Blanchard around the carnival grounds. But as they approached the booths, the decorations and displays disappeared before his eyes, just like the words on the mysterious messages. Soon all the booths were empty.

In his dream, the Vice President turned to him and said, "Oh, Mr. Lyle, this is such a disappointment. I thought I was invited to a carnival. But all I see are a lot of empty booths."

"I'm sorry," said Mr. Lyle.

"You will be," said the Vice President. "This will be on television. All the newspapers will print it."

"But why?" cried Mr. Lyle. "This is just Hillcrest Junior High School. Who cares?"

"When you invite the Vice President, everybody cares. The whole country will be laughing at you."

Mr. Lyle woke up in a cold sweat. "Maybe I have been working too hard," he whispered in the dark.

The next morning Mr. Lyle expected to see more blue pieces of paper, but to his relief, he found none. "I must have imagined the messages disappearing," he said. "Someone must have been playing a trick on me, handing out blank pieces of paper. Whoever it was, I don't think it was funny."

As he locked up the Rolls Royce, Professor, Doc, and Mary Jane casually strolled up to him.

"Good morning, Mr. Lyle," Professor said, "we'd like a word with you."

"What about?"

"The carnival."

"I told your friend yesterday I didn't want to discuss it."

"But we just found out that there is an empty booth," said Professor.

"The carnival is less than a week away," said Mary Jane. "It might be hard to find someone who would have a display ready in time."

"And we already have something," said Doc.

"That paint thing—that P-4 whatchamacallit is out. Definitely out! It's too dangerous," said Mr. Lyle.

"We've got something else," said Professor. "It doesn't involve paint. This is a way to catch criminals. It's a detection device called NOSE and EARS. It smells and listens."

"Smells!" exclaimed Mr. Lyle. "You kids would probably start squirting skunk oil all over the place."

"No, we wouldn't. Honest!" said Mary Jane. "It doesn't have any moving parts. It's really very safe."

"And," Doc added, "we could fill the empty booth."

The words *fill the empty booth* made Mr. Lyle vividly recall his nightmare. Surely, *one* empty booth wouldn't matter. But still, with the Vice President there and all, maybe it would be better to be extra careful. A look of defeat crossed Mr. Lyle's face.

"There's a booth half started. It's way at the far edge of the carnival near that old shed by the back gate," Mr. Lyle said. "Are you sure you could finish it in time?"

"Absolutely!" said Mary Jane.

"It's yours, then," said Mr. Lyle. "Just make sure it's safe."

"Thank you, Mr. Lyle," said Professor with a big smile on his face. "When shall we show you our entry?"

"Never," said Mr. Lyle. "Show it to Mrs. Stern." And he headed toward the school building, leaving three very happy students behind.

10   EARS HEARS

It was two days before the carnival. Doc, Mary Jane, Cookie, and Professor were at the school yard working on the booth. TJ was in the treehouse. She had wakened that morning with a fever, and her mother insisted that she stay home from school.

"Please let me go, Mom," TJ begged. "I feel okay. Honest, I do."

But she had chills and felt so dizzy when she stood up that TJ knew her mother was right. When her mother took her temperature with the analytical thermometer, the printout read, "Mild case of flu. You will be better in exactly 21½ hours."

"Oh good," said TJ, "at least I can go to school tomorrow."

The analytical thermometer continued, "Only if you stay in bed until noon. You can go to the treehouse at 12:30 if you wear a sweater."

TJ made a face. How boring to have to stay in bed all morning. However, her mother insisted, warning her, "If you don't take care of yourself today, Tilda Jean, you may get worse, and that would mean you'd have to miss the carnival completely."

TJ knew her mother was right. And so she spent the morning in bed, watching television and drinking hot tea and being mean and grumbly the whole time.

At exactly 12:30, she threw off the covers, tore out of her pajamas, dashed into her clothes, and magnabeamed up to the treehouse by 12:32. But what a surprise she found! Everything that had been in the treehouse was now out on the platform. Bartholomew had picked this day to do a massive cleaning job.

The treehouse wasn't very large, and wherever TJ started to sit, she seemed to be just where Bartholomew was dusting or washing. Finally, he took her by the arm and guided her to the platform where Poindexter, trying to make himself as inconspicuous as possible, was reading one of his usual mysteries.

TJ cleared away some of the chemistry equipment, leaned NOSE and EARS carefully against the railing, and made a small space for herself so she could sit down beside Poindexter. But it was clear from his attitude that he wasn't interested in carrying on a conversation with her.

From where she sat on the treehouse platform, TJ could see the street. Her house was on the parade route, and TJ leaned her elbows on the railing and tried to imagine what it would be like when the Vice President rode by two days from then.

All of a sudden TJ noticed that NOSE's red light was on. "When had *that* happened?" she wondered. She glanced down at the street. Except for one car slowly passing by, there was no one in sight at all.

"I wonder if we got NOSE right after all. That car has Secret Service written on its side. Those guys can't be crooks."

But TJ put on the earphones and listened.

"Then we can grab her," she heard a man's voice say.

"Right," said another man's voice, "since we've infiltrated the Secret Service so successfully, no one will suspect us."

"What are they talking about? Who are they going to grab?" wondered TJ as she frantically tried to search for the tape recorder and listen at the same time. There was a lot of static coming through the earphones and TJ wasn't able to hear

72

very clearly, but she was sure she heard the words *the Vice President* at least twice.

"Oh, golly," said TJ. She put her hand to her head. She couldn't believe what she had just heard. "It sounds like a plot to kidnap the Vice President. I've got to find out more about this."

She grabbed NOSE and EARS and magnabeamed down from the treehouse. "I've got to follow that car. I've got to get their license plate at least. I've got to . . . "

She made it just outside the gate and then she heard, "Tilda Jean! Tilda Jean, where are you going?"

"Can't stop now, Mom, this is important."

"And so is your health, young lady. You come back here this minute!"

Even if TJ had been able to convince her mother to let her continue, it wouldn't have done any good. The car was out of sight.

TJ trudged dejectedly back to her house. What was she going to do, now? How would she be able to convince anybody about what she had heard?

Tilda Jean's mother wouldn't let her see the others until the twenty-one and a half hours were up, but TJ was able to arrange a conference call on the videophone as soon as the others came home from school.

"Are you sure that's what you heard?" Doc asked.

"Absolutely," said TJ.

"And you're positive it's the Vice President they're planning to kidnap?" asked Professor.

"Yes," said TJ.

"Maybe that's why I had that funny feeling something bad was going to happen at the carnival. Maybe this is what the bad thing is going to be," said Doc.

"How do you feel, now?" asked Professor.

"Cold and shivery," said Doc.

"Wow!" said Cookie. "What do you think we should do next?"

73

"I think we ought to go straight to the police," said Mary Jane.

"I somehow don't think they're going to believe us," said Doc.

"Of course they will. We're law-abiding citizens, and this is something important," Mary Jane told them.

"I don't know," Doc's voice was doubtful.

"I'm afraid we don't have much choice," said Professor. "But let's think about it until tomorrow. We can't go until then because TJ can't leave her house, and she's our star witness."

"When can you leave?" asked Cookie.

"At 8:30 tomorrow morning," said TJ.

"It's a good thing the day before the carnival is a school holiday," said Mary Jane. "That way we won't have to miss school."

"All right," said Professor. "We'll meet in front of TJ's at 8:30 tomorrow, and we'll all go to the police together. In the meantime, TJ, write down everything you can remember."

11　THE COPS COP OUT

"We've got to see someone in charge," said TJ, as soon as they got to the police station.

"What about?" asked the sergeant at the desk.

"It's the Vice President," said Professor.

"We think they're planning to kidnap her," said TJ.

"Wait a minute! Wait a minute! Who's going to kidnap the Vice President?" asked the sergeant.

"The Secret Service," said TJ. "We heard it through EARS."

By now there were three more police officers watching this scene.

"What do you mean, through your ears?" asked one of them. "How else would you hear, through your nose?"

"Oh, no," said Cookie. "NOSE smells and then lights up."

"What are you? Some kind of wise guy?" the sergeant asked Cookie.

Mary Jane explained. "This is EARS, and this is NOSE," she told them, pointing to each piece of equipment.

"I'd never have known if you hadn't told me," laughed one of the police officers. "This looks like a cigar box, and this looks like a large ice cream cone."

"Never mind how they look," said Doc. "It's what they do that's important."

"And what might that be?" asked another officer.

"NOSE stands for Negative Odor Sensing Equipment," said TJ, "and if it smells out a combination of sweat, metal, and gunpowder, then its red light goes on."

"That activates EARS—Electronic Auditory Receiving System," said Mary Jane. "EARS can hear things within a half-mile radius, but it only works when it's attached to NOSE."

"NOSE and EARS were conceived on the theory that people who are planning to commit crimes would be apprehensive, causing them to perspire. It additionally takes into consideration that they would also carry weaponry as part of their equipage," added Professor.

"Does he always use those big words?" asked an officer.

"Only when he's saying something that's very important," Doc explained.

"Let me finish," said Mary Jane. "TJ and Professor . . . "

"He must be Professor," interrupted the officer, pointing at the proper person.

"TJ was in our treehouse," continued Mary Jane, trying very hard to make the police pay attention. "She overheard two men talking in a car. They said that they had infiltrated the Secret Service. They mentioned the words *the Vice President*."

"At least twice," said TJ. "I have an excellent memory, and I wrote it all down." She handed the sergeant a piece of paper, but he waved it aside impatiently.

"We're busy today, kids," he said. "The Vice President is coming for the carnival. We're planning for her visit."

"We know she's coming," TJ said. "We think she's going to be kidnapped."

"Tell us another time," said the sergeant.

76

The Fabulous Five looked at each other in dismay.

They couldn't figure out how it had happened. Here they had come to the police to report a possible serious crime, and nobody would pay any attention to them.

It wasn't fair. No wonder they were confused and angry. In fact, Doc got so angry that she lost her voice, as she often did in situations such as this. She began waving her arms around.

"Of course," said Professor who could understand exactly what she meant. "Your assessment of this situation is accurate. Your proposed solution is more than feasible."

Professor turned to the sergeant and said, "Why don't you let us demonstrate NOSE and EARS? When you see that they work, it will prove that we are telling the truth about everything."

The sergeant thought this over for a moment, and then said, "Why not?"

The Fabulous Five started turning NOSE and EARS in all directions. Unfortunately, there were no crooks in the station house at the time. There were only police officers. So even though there were guns and gunpowder, the third element was missing. There was no sweat because the officers were not nervous.

"We've got to do something," whispered TJ.

"Maybe we could ask them to turn up the heat. At least, then they would perspire. And NOSE and EARS would start working," said Mary Jane.

"Capital idea," said Professor.

But when they asked the sergeant to do this, he only laughed. "We've gone along with your gag far enough," he said. "Now beat it, kids, we're busy."

"But . . . but . . . but . . ." said TJ.

"I said, beat it kids. We police officers have no more time for clowning around."

"Come on guys," said Doc. "I hate to say I told you so, but . . ."

Just then a police officer who had just arrived asked someone what was going on. When he heard the story, he whispered to the sergeant, "I don't believe this NOSE and EARS junk, but I think we ought to think it over. Just suppose that they did hear something? Don't you think we should call the Secret Service to check it out just in case? We sure would be in a lot of trouble if they turned out to be right and we ignored them."

The sergeant considered this advice. "I suppose it couldn't do any harm," he said. "I'll go right to the top."

He checked his special telephone book for the number of the Secret Service in Washington. Everyone waited impatiently. He dialed the number.

"Hello, Secret Service?" he asked. "Give me the chief. No, I can't talk to anybody else. This could be urgent."

It seemed forever until he reached him.

"Hello, Chief? This is Sergeant Sweeney in Hillcrest, California. You know the Vice President is coming to our carnival tomorrow? Well, there's a bunch of kids here who say there are two men posing as Secret Service agents who are probably going to kidnap her. They overheard part of a conversation, they say. I just wanted to let you know."

The group in the police station could only hear one end of the conversation because the sergeant had chosen not to use the videophone. All they could hear Sergeant Sweeney say was, "uh huh . . . uh huh . . . uh huh . . . All right . . . Thanks a lot . . . just thought I'd pass it on so you would know about it . . . Sorry to bother you."

He hung up the phone. He turned to the group. "You all heard me call Washington, D.C., just now and talk to the head of the Secret Service. He says that they always have every agent accounted for, and that scheme would be impossible."

"But I heard these men say no one knew they had infiltrated the Secret Service," said TJ.

"Look, kid," Sergeant Sweeney was clearly getting impatient now, "maybe your EARS heard wrong. Maybe you got tuned in on some TV program by mistake."

"But . . . " TJ started to protest, but the sergeant cut her short. "No buts, kid. The chances of your story being true are maybe one in a billion, if even that. Now, if I were positive that you kids were telling the truth, I'd send one of my officers here to check around a bit. But I think you kids are down here on a dare, or a joke, or something."

The sergeant looked very stern and pointed his finger at them before continuing, "But in case—mind you—just in case you're not, I've got to check up on you to see if you're reliable or jokers. If you're reliable, we might check into it a little bit more. What're your names, kids?"

They told him their names, and he carefully wrote this information down on a pad of paper.

"And what school do you go to?"

"Hillcrest Junior High."

"Oh? Mr. Lyle's school."

The Fabulous Five nodded their heads. "Well," said the sergeant, "Mr. Lyle happens to be a friend of mine. Since today is a school holiday, I'll give him a call at home and tell him who you are. If he says you're okay, we'll check out your story a little further. Is that fair?"

The Fabulous Five looked at one another. They all knew how they stood with Mr. Lyle, but they didn't have any choice in the matter. They couldn't tell Sergeant Sweeney not to call him.

"Sure, go ahead," said TJ swallowing hard.

The Sergeant dialed Mr. Lyle's number and then said, "Mr. Lyle? I hate to bother you, but this is Sergeant Sweeney at the police station. I have five of your students here who are telling me a story about the Vice President being kidnapped, and I wanted to check them out for character references."

The sergeant paused for a moment, listening. Then he said, "Why don't you turn on your videophone, and I'll turn

79

on mine so you can see them yourself."

Everyone in the station house could see Mr. Lyle's expression as he recognized the Fabulous Five.

"Turn off the videophone, sergeant," they could hear him say. "I'll tell you the rest of this in private."

"You don't say?" the sergeant said, frowning. He listened some more. "They did *that*?"

The Fabulous Five could pretty well figure out what Mr. Lyle was telling the sergeant, who was listening very intently.

"She did? The skinny one with the braids and thick glasses?" the sergeant asked with a shocked look on his face. "Well, thanks a lot, Mr. Lyle. I'm sorry to have disturbed you. I guess we got our answer now."

He hung up the phone and shook his head slowly. "I'm not going to repeat all of what Mr. Lyle said, but I guess you got the general idea. You kids had better leave quietly before I take Mr. Lyle's suggestion and keep you here for a much longer visit."

"But, sergeant," TJ began.

"No buts!" said Sergeant Sweeney. "We're too busy to have you kids in here, interrupting us as we help protect the law-abiding citizens of Hillcrest against crime. Beat it! All of you! And don't be playing tricks on the police department again!"

"Wow!" said Cookie, as soon as they got out of there. "What are we going to do now?"

"Go back to the treehouse," said TJ. "We've got to do some serious thinking."

12 SAM THE SNITCH SNOOPS

"**W**ait," said TJ, not more than a block from the police station. "We'd better go to the treehouse separately."

"What for?" asked Cookie.

"Looks a lot less suspicious that way," said TJ.

"Suspicious? Who's going to be suspicious of us?" asked Mary Jane.

"Sergeant Sweeney called the Secret Service, didn't he?" asked TJ. "Suppose somebody back there is working with the men who are planning the kidnapping? If they think we know something, they might come after us."

"Do you think we're going to be kidnapped, too?" asked Cookie.

"Or murdered?" asked Mary Jane. "I'm getting scared."

"It's unwise to let our imaginations intimidate us," said Professor. "Conversely, TJ's recommendation that we exercise a reasonable amount of caution is a prudent one."

"In other words," said Doc. "Don't be scared. But be careful."

"Exactly," agreed Professor. "I couldn't have said it better myself."

"Take different routes," said TJ. "And make sure nobody's following you."

★★★★★

"We've got to do something about making this place more secure," said TJ when everyone had arrived.

"What we need is a guard," said Cookie.

"How about a watchdog?" suggested Professor.

"My mother won't let me have a dog," said TJ. "Besides, she'd get pretty worried if she thought we were in danger. She might even make us stop meeting here."

"Maybe we can keep Bartholomew on duty all the time," said Doc. "He could drop a net on anyone bad who comes around."

"That's what I was thinking," said TJ. "The only problem is that his power supply is limited."

"There must be some way to extend it," said Mary Jane.

"I looked for my father's notes about Bartholomew, but I couldn't find them," said TJ.

"Can't you call him up and ask him?" Cookie wondered.

TJ gave him a withering look. "Do you know how much it costs to call Jupiter? He told me the only time I could call him was if there was a really super big emergency." She shook her head. "We'll have to figure this one out for ourselves."

Mary Jane took Bartholomew down from the wall and examined the mechanism implanted in his chest.

"TJ," she asked, "couldn't we add a perennial-power solarcircuit?"

"I guess that would work," TJ replied. "But he's so small. I don't know where we'd put it."

"Under here," Mary Jane said, removing Bartholomew's long pointy hat.

"Oh!" she exclaimed in surprise. "Bartholomew's head

82

comes to a point! It's exactly the same shape as his hat! Why was he built that way?"

"So his hat would stay on," said TJ. "You can see there's no room there for the solarcircuit at all."

"We could implant it in his head," said Mary Jane.

"Surgery?" asked TJ. A flicker of indecision crossed her face.

"Is it dangerous?" asked Professor.

"It would take a lot of skill," said TJ.

"You know how good I am with tools," said Mary Jane. "I can do it."

TJ hesitated. But only for a second. "I know you can," she said. "Let's go."

Doc and Cookie covered the table with a clean white cloth and gently laid Bartholomew on it, face down.

"He looks so helpless," Cookie said.

Mary Jane put on a fresh pair of pink coveralls, tied back her blonde curls in a pink scarf, and pulled on a pair of sterile gloves. Professor held the generator in case Bartholomew needed an emergency power transfusion. TJ, also wearing sterile gloves, held the perennial-power solarcircuit in a pair of tweezers, ready to hand it to Mary Jane when she needed it.

Even Poindexter put down his book and came to watch.

"No talking, please," said Mary Jane. "I need to concentrate."

No one said a word, but when she took the miniature saw and made the first cut into Bartholomew's head, Cookie let out a loud gasp.

"Quiet," Mary Jane commanded. "If you're going to faint, go outside."

Mary Jane quickly cut a square incision into which she implanted the solarcircuit. Using tools no larger than a fingernail, she made the necessary connections. Then she closed the flap so skillfully that the scar was invisible.

"Now let's try his power," Mary Jane said, turning Bartholomew on his back and replacing his hat.

TJ activated Bartholomew's on button.

The light on Bartholomew's hat flickered slowly. His eyelids fluttered open. He turned his head from side to side.

Bartholomew sat up. He wiggled to the edge of the table and carefully jumped off. He brushed off the white cloth, folded it neatly, and put it away.

Then Bartholomew took his broom and swept under the table. The light on the top of his hat was shining brightly.

"That was good work, Mary Jane," said TJ.

Mary Jane smiled. "I knew I could do it," she said.

"Now that Bartholomew's on guard, we've got to do something about finding those phony Secret Service men," said TJ.

"It's going to be hard. We don't know what they look like. We don't have the license number of their car. All we have is TJ's recollection of part of a conversation she overheard," said Doc.

Cookie was looking through the yellow pages of the telephone directory. "Boy, there sure are a lot of hotels and motels listed here," he said.

"Why are you interested in hotels and motels?" asked Mary Jane.

"Well," said Cookie. "I thought we could call up and try to find out where those Secret Service guys are staying and then take NOSE and EARS over and try to find out what their plans are."

"It's a good idea, but we don't even know their names," said Doc.

"Maybe we could call and just ask for the Secret Service," said Cookie.

"You know they'll never admit they're there," said Mary Jane. "Why do you suppose they're called secret?"

"One moment, please," said Professor. "Let's assume that the Secret Service gentlemen will want to headquarter themselves in close proximity to the carnival. I've been glancing through a list of temporary lodgings, and there seem to be only two of them close to the school, the Hillcrest Hotel on Hillcrest Road and the Maple Street Motel on Maple Street. I suggest we position ourselves in front of each of them with NOSE and EARS and see if NOSE lights up."

"What if it doesn't?" asked Mary Jane.

Professor shrugged his shoulders. "Then we try something else."

"I say we go ahead with this. It's our only idea, and the carnival is tomorrow," said TJ.

They tried the Hillcrest Hotel first and stayed there for an hour. No luck. NOSE did not light up.

Then they hurried over to Maple Street and waited in front of the Maple Street Motel.

"Suppose they've gone out," said Mary Jane. "Suppose they're not carrying guns."

"Suppose! Suppose! Suppose! Don't be so negative, Mary Jane," snapped Doc. "We've got to do the best we can, and you're not making it any better by your whining."

She saw the look on Mary Jane's face. "I'm sorry," Doc quickly apologized. "I'm so keyed up about this, my nerves are edgy."

"I guess we're all that way," said Mary Jane.

"You wouldn't be if you ate enough," said Cookie. "I'm as calm as you can be as long as I have my . . . "

Cookie looked around. "Where are my cookies?" he asked.

He spied a brown paper bag. "TJ! Did you sit on my cookies?" He opened it up. "You did sit on my cookies. Now all I've got are crumbs. Why don't you ever. . . "

"Calm, calm, calm," said Doc, but the woebegone expression on Cookie's face was enough to make everyone burst out laughing. And whenever there was laughter, Cookie always joined in.

"Have some crummy cookies," he said, passing around the bag. But no sooner had he said that when NOSE's warning light turned on. The cookies were immediately forgotten as the Fabulous Five sprang into action.

TJ grabbed the earphones.

"It's them," she said excitedly. "I recognize their voices."

But almost as soon as she said that, she frowned. "Where's the sound? I can't hear anything."

She put her hand to the earphones. She looked around angrily. There was Sam the Snitch with his hand clamped tightly over the cone-shaped portion of NOSE. Doc had grabbed his arm, trying to make him let go, but Sam was holding on tighter than ever. If he jerked his arm back, he might just tear that part of EARS off.

"Hey, let go of me!" said Sam.

"Give that to me," said Doc.

"I will when you guys tell me what you're doing," Sam said.

"Saaammmmm," said TJ. Her voice was cold and deadly.

"Okay, okay," he said hastily, removing his hand from the receiving end of EARS.

TJ listened intently, but it was no use. The would-be kidnappers had stopped talking.

"No luck," said TJ, "they've stopped." Her whole body drooped with dejection.

"All right, Sam, what do you want?" asked Professor.

"I was just walking by, and I saw you guys. And I thought I'd just come over and be friendly," he told them.

"Thanks a lot," said Doc.

"Yeah, we really appreciate it," said Cookie.

"And I wanted to tell you that I've got my carnival exhibit all finished. It's a hot air balloon," Sam said.

"That figures," murmured Professor.

"It's right near the entrance, where the Vice President will be sure to notice it," Sam continued.

TJ had not taken the earphones off. Suddenly, she heard some faint sounds, as though they were coming back into the room. TJ leaned forward, straining to hear. The others leaned forward to watch her. All except Sam, who was oblivious to everything except his own story.

"Of course it's not a full size hot air balloon," Sam was saying. "That would take up too much space. It's a half size model. But it still can fly. I plan to hover gently over the carnival, and . . ."

TJ had put her finger over her lips and pointed to Sam.

"Sam," Professor said, "please be quiet. TJ's trying to listen over the earphones, and she can't because you're talking."

"Sorry," said Sam. "What's she listening to?"

"We don't know," said Professor. "I'm sure she'll tell us afterwards."

"I'd like to listen, too," said Sam. "You know how interested I am in everything that goes on. Do you think she'd let me?"

And without waiting for an answer, Sam the Snitch walked over and lifted the earphones from TJ's head.

"Let me hear, too, TJ," he said.

TJ grabbed for the earphones. Sam stepped back. The earphones snapped out of their connecting socket.

"Now look what you've done," TJ yelled. "Give them back right now!"

"I just wanted to try them. I'll let you guys ride in my balloon if you're nice. I don't know why you can't be more friendly."

Sam started backing off. The Fabulous Five surrounded him. Sam saw the menacing looks on their faces. He hastily handed the earphones to TJ.

TJ plugged them in. There was no sound anymore. She groaned.

Cookie turned to Sam the Snitch. "You've done enough for today, Sam. You'd better get moving."

"I can go wherever I want . . ." Sam started to say, but five pairs of steely eyes stared at him. "I was just trying to be friendly," Sam said lamely.

Ten fists shook at him.

"I guess I better go now," Sam said. "See you around." He carefully backed to the corner, keeping a wary eye on the

Fabulous Five. As soon as he reached the corner, however, he turned and ran as fast as he could.

"Oh, darn it all!" said TJ. "That crumb-bum Sam came along and ruined everything! Now we're practically right back where we started."

"Did you hear anything?" asked Professor.

"Not much at all. They said something about things would start happening at two o'clock." said TJ. "But they didn't say what."

"It must be the kidnapping," said Cookie. "That's probably when they plan to grab her."

"Maybe," said TJ, shrugging her shoulders dejectedly. "I just don't know."

"Maybe they'll come back and talk some more and we can get some more clues," said Doc.

"I doubt it," said TJ. "I heard them say that they wouldn't be back until late. Then I heard the sound of the door closing. There's no chance at all."

The sun was starting to set.

"We'd better go home now," said Mary Jane. "It'll be time for dinner soon."

"I'm not even hungry," said Cookie. "That's how upset I am." Doc patted him on the back in sympathy.

"I guess we had all better go home," said TJ. "One way or the other, we've got a busy day tomorrow."

13 THE CARNIVAL CAPER COMMENCES

The morning of the carnival was clear and bright. It was going to be a hot day; anyone could tell that. But still Doc felt cold and shivery. Cookie noticed it when they were walking over to the treehouse.

"Are you sure you're not catching the flu, Doc?" Cookie asked.

"Positive. I took my temperature on the analytical thermometer, and there's absolutely nothing wrong with me except my feeling that something bad is going to happen."

"I sure hope you're wrong," said Cookie.

"Me, too," Doc agreed gloomily.

Cookie and Doc were the last to arrive at the treehouse. Everyone looked super. Mary Jane's newest pink dress had buttons that sparkled. Professor's hair wasn't falling in his eyes. Cookie had tucked his shirt into his trousers. Doc's clothes were ironed. TJ had even changed from the grubby jeans she usually wore, and her hair was neatly braided.

Professor put NOSE and EARS under his arm. They were ready to magnabeam down when Doc said, "We have to take the P-4, too. And plenty of extra paint."

"We can't," said Mary Jane. "You know what Mr. Lyle said."

"I know what Mr. Lyle said," Doc answered impatiently. "But my ESP is saying something else. My ESP says take it."

"But if Mr. Lyle sees the P-4, he's liable to kick us out of the carnival completely," said Mary Jane.

"I've got an idea," said Professor. "Mr. Lyle said we couldn't have the P-4 in the carnival. Well, we're so close to the back gate of the school yard, we could just leave it outside. That way, we could get to it fast if we need it."

"Mr. Lyle couldn't object to that," said Mary Jane.

"Mr. Lyle doesn't even have to know about it," said TJ.

"I think it's a darn good idea," said Cookie.

They all decided it would be a suitable compromise, and Doc began to stop shivering.

The Fabulous Five were at their booth well before noon. The students had transformed an ordinary school yard into a festive carnival. Balloons and flags were everywhere. Large crepe paper flowers decorated the booths. A big red and gold banner stretched across the entrance and read "Hillcrest Junior High Welcomes You."

The nylaplex shelter had been moved from its usual place at the front gate to a new one right beside the speaker's platform.

Anyone who had a booth in the carnival had to be there long before it started, so they weren't able to watch the parade.

But they could hear the music getting closer.

They could hear the cheering getting louder.

The Hillcrest Junior High School marching band tried to enter the school yard in orderly rows. But the spectators mingled with them as they approached the carnival site, causing great disorder. Piccolos marched with clarinets; trumpets with drums.

Sam, who had the best view of all from his hot air balloon, shouted progress reports to those below him.

"She's just coming through the gate now," he called.

People surged toward the yellow Rolls Royce, reaching

out to shake Ms. Blanchard's hand. Mr. Lyle, who was driving, pressed hard on the horn, trying to clear a path. The two Secret Service men who had been riding in the back seat leapt from the car and walked beside it, one on each side, trying to hold the crowd back.

As the car inched toward the school steps, NOSE lit up.

"Is that them?" asked Cookie.

"I don't know," said TJ, who had the earphones on. "I can't hear anything because of the background noise."

"Maybe it's just a false alarm," said Mary Jane. "Maybe they're sweating because it's so hot."

"I can't tell yet," said TJ impatiently. "We're going to have to wait and see."

The Vice President got out of the car. She was wearing a white dress and carrying a large bunch of red roses. A welcoming committee—the Mayor of Hillcrest, the President of the Hillcrest Junior High School PTA, and the Hillcrest Junior High School Student Council Carnival Chairperson—were waiting in a line to greet her.

Mr. Lyle quickly parked the Rolls Royce in its nylaplex shelter and hurried to the school steps. He held up both hands for silence.

"Welcome to the carnival, everyone," he shouted into the portamike. "I'm sure that you all know what a tremendous amount of work the students of Hillcrest Junior High put into it."

A few *yeas* and a smattering of applause were heard.

"Our carnival is always a special occasion, and this year is no exception. We have with us a wonderful guest—Ms. Helen Blanchard, the Vice President of the United States."

This statement prompted louder cheers from the crowd.

Mr. Lyle smiled. "We have with us today to introduce Ms. Blanchard none other than his honor, Adam T. Franklin, Mayor of Hillcrest."

Mayor Franklin came forward, took a stack of notes from his pocket, cleared his throat, and began. "Ladies and gentlemen, fair citizens of the town of Hillcrest, and our most gracious and honored guest, Ms. Blanchard."

The mayor cleared his throat and looked down at his notes. "As long as there has been a Hillcrest Junior High School, there has been a Hillcrest Junior High School annual carnival. I went here myself as a boy. Of course, that was long before Ms. Blanchard."

Mayor Franklin chuckled, then glanced at his notes. "I remember the carnivals we used to have—in the good old days." And he launched into a long—and very boring—speech. Young children tugged at their parents' hands and asked when the carnival was going to start. Adults coughed and shuffled their feet. Even Mr. Lyle put his hand over his mouth several times to cover yawns.

Finally, just when it seemed he would never finish, Mayor Franklin read from the last of his notes. "And now, it is my great pleasure to introduce our guest of honor, Ms. Helen Blanchard."

A loud and enthusiastic cheer went up, as much to applaud the end of the mayor's speech as to welcome the Vice President.

"I'm delighted to be here with you today," she began. "Mayor Franklin has said so many things that I shall keep my remarks brief." Very loud applause greeted this statement.

"As I look around, I notice that, although there have been some changes in the campus, the friendliness of the people hasn't changed at all. Now what I would really like to see is whether the carnival is anything like it was when I was a student here. I hope you enjoy yourselves. I know I will."

At this remark, Mr. Lyle offered the Vice President his arm. And off they went, closely followed by the two Secret Service men.

Their first stop was at Sam's hot air balloon. Although the balloon had a line that would enable it to rise fifty feet into the air, it was firmly anchored down so that it rose no more than four feet.

Mr. Lyle introduced Sam to the Vice President. Sam leaned

over and shook hands. He offered to take her for a ride, but she thanked him politely, telling him that she had too many other exhibits to look at.

By now it was 1:42. NOSE's red light was still on. The Vice President walked from booth to booth, shaking hands with the students and talking to them. A large crowd had gathered around her and followed wherever she went.

TJ was straining to hear anything that the Secret Service men might say to see if she could recognize their voices. But there was so much noise it was impossible.

"Maybe we could leave our booth and go follow them with NOSE and EARS," said TJ.

"We can't do that," said Mary Jane. "Mr. Lyle said that we all have to stay in our booths as long as the Vice President is at the carnival."

"Yeah," said Cookie. "Suppose she decided to come over here to look at our booth, and it was empty."

"I wouldn't worry about that happening," said TJ. "Fat chance that Mr. Lyle will let her get any place near us."

"I'm afraid that is a correct assumption," Professor agreed. "We're so far away from most of the carnival that she'd need a compass to find us."

"But you're wrong," said Doc, "because they're coming this way. Look!"

As the crowd came closer, TJ could barely hear Mr. Lyle say to the Vice President, "You've seen just about every booth here today. I don't think that you'll find this one very interesting."

They could see the Vice President smile and nod her head. "But I would like to, Mr. Lyle," she said. "I want to see every booth and talk to everybody who's taking part in the carnival."

TJ hastily took the earphones off as they approached. As much as she wanted to listen, she knew it would be rude to keep them on. When Mr. Lyle and the Vice President got to the booth, Mr Lyle introduced the Fabulous Five to Ms. Blanchard.

After she shook their hands and complimented them on how nicely their booth was decorated, Ms. Blanchard said, "Please tell me about your entry."

Mr. Lyle looked as though he had swallowed a raw egg, shell and all. But before any of the Fabulous Five could reply, one of the Secret Service men came up and whispered to the Vice President, "I don't mean to hurry you, ma'am. But we do have to head back to the plane now."

"Oh," she answered, glancing at her watch. "I hadn't realized how late it was." She turned to the Fabulous Five. "I'm sorry that I don't have time. We're on such a tight schedule that practically every second counts."

Then she smiled at Mr. Lyle and shook his hand. "Thank you for the wonderful ride in your beautiful car," she said. "I wish I were going back in that instead of the official limousine."

"It's time, ma'am," the Secret Service man reminded her once more.

"Of course," she said. "Thank you all again," she called to the people nearby. Waving to the crowd, she walked toward the school yard entrance where the limousine was parked.

"Are those the ones?" asked Mary Jane. "Do you recognize their voices?"

"I don't think so," TJ said.

"Let's get closer then," said Doc.

"I'll leave NOSE and EARS here," said TJ. "It's just too noisy for them to work properly."

They left their booth and headed toward the car. As the Vice President was about to step into it, two other men came out of the crowd. They were dressed just like the Secret Service men with the Vice President.

"We'll take over now," one of the new men said.

"What the . . . " a Secret Service man started to ask.

But the two newcomers swiftly hit the two original Secret Service men on the head with their guns, knocking them to the ground.

94

Meanwhile, the driver of the car had rushed out, grabbed the Vice President, and held one of his arms around her neck while he aimed a pistol at the crowd with his other hand.

"Don't anybody come any closer," he warned. "If anybody tries to harm us, then we're going to hurt her."

14 THE CARNIVAL CAPER CONTINUES

And with those words, he pushed the Vice President into the car. As soon as he was in the driver's seat, the two other men jumped into the car themselves.

When she saw what happened to the first Secret Service men, TJ motioned to the others to duck down and follow her. Since everybody else's eyes were riveted on the scene with the Vice President, no one noticed the Fabulous Five slithering toward the back gate.

"Grab as much paint as you can carry and follow me," said TJ, scooping up the Perfect Portable Personality Painter in her arms.

She swiftly led them around to the entrance to the playground. The limousine carrying the Vice President was slowly heading their way. Someone had turned on the car's loudspeaker.

"Stand back! Stand back!" a harsh voice blared. "If anybody tries to stop us, we will hurt Ms. Blanchard. We will make an announcement at four o'clock. Stand back! Stand back!"

The crowd slowly parted. The car inched forward.

"We've got to cover their windshield with paint," said TJ. "If the driver can't see, then he'll have to stop. We'll rush in, puncture the tires, and save the Vice President. Now—ready, aim, fire!"

Blobs of color splattered the windshield, the hood, the roof. But instead of stopping, the driver made a U-turn and headed back toward the school grounds. The car seemed out of control, lurching from side to side. People, afraid of being hit, were running away in all directions. The driver knocked over a booth full of giant red and yellow paper flowers. The flowers stuck to the wet paint that covered the car. The driver still didn't stop.

"It didn't work," said Mary Jane. "What'll we do now?"

"I've got another idea," said TJ. She ran over to Sam the Snitch, who was hovering above the carnival, still avidly watching everything that was happening.

"Hey, Sam! Catch!" TJ shouted, tossing him the P-4.

"What's it for?" he asked.

"You'll see in a minute. Just shake it up good and hold it out in front of you," she said, swiftly letting out the rope that held Sam's hot air balloon four feet from the ground. The balloon soared to fifty feet, dancing merrily on the early afternoon breeze.

"What are you doing, TJ?" Sam shrieked. "Help! Help! Help me, someone. I'm flying! Help! Help! HELP!"

In his excitement, Sam almost dropped the P-4 over the side.

"Don't drop that, Sam," shouted TJ. "Whatever you do, DON'T DROP THAT!"

Without thinking, Sam reacted by hugging the P-4 close to his chest. The sudden jolt was all that was needed to turn the P-4 on.

Paint started spraying in all directions.

Sam ducked down into the gondola of the hot air balloon,

holding the P-4 at arm's length to keep from getting covered with paint himself.

By now, people were pushing each other to get out of the school yard. Mr. Lyle was standing on the school steps, his arms outstretched, yelling, "Be calm everybody! Be calm!"

But nobody was paying the least bit of attention to him. Parents were scooping up young children in their arms. All the dogs for miles around were barking. People who lived in the neighborhood were swarming out to see what was going on.

Sam the Snitch was floating over the carnival in his hot air balloon with the P-4 shooting rainbows of paint everywhere. The balloon hovered over Mr. Lyle. The P-4 was aimed.

"Oh, no!" shouted Mr. Lyle, trying to duck. "Get out of here!" he screamed.

But to no avail. Mr. Lyle was covered with bright orange from head to toe. He sat down on the school steps and put his head in his hands.

The car with the Vice President in it had just bumped into one of the poles holding the large red and gold banner reading: Hillcrest Junior High Welcomes You. It was now flundering around with the banner draped over it.

The car headed toward the school steps. One kidnapper got out and spoke to Mr. Lyle.

Across the school yard Doc caught a glimpse of what was happening. She sensed trouble. She quickly climbed on top of a booth to get a clearer picture.

"We need your car," the kidnapper said.

"My car!" gasped Mr. Lyle. "Oh, no! no! no!"

"This gun says, 'yes,' " said the kidnapper, showing his weapon.

Mr. Lyle argued no further. The kidnapper grabbed him by the arm, practically dragged him to the nylaplex shelter, and made him unlock it. Mr. Lyle climbed into the Rolls Royce. He put the key in the ignition. He started to turn it, and then he slumped over the steering wheel.

"Get moving," said the kidnapper. "Get the car out of here."

"I can't," moaned Mr. Lyle. "I don't know what the matter is. I can't move. I'm in pain."

"You've got to move."

"I can't," moaned Mr. Lyle again.

The kidnapper bent over Mr. Lyle to check what was the matter. Mr. Lyle jerked up his fist and socked the kidnapper in the jaw.

"Aha!" Mr. Lyle said. "Fooled you, didn't I? I'm a better actor than most people give me credit for."

Mr. Lyle leapt from the car and started running. The kidnapper, who was only momentarily stunned, started off in hot pursuit.

Doc had seen enough. "Mr. Lyle is in trouble," she shouted to the others as she scrambled down from the top of the booth.

"Well, let somebody else rescue him. We've got more important things to do," said TJ.

"We've got to help him, TJ," said Professor. "We've sworn to do good deeds."

"Oh, all right," TJ grumbled. "But it's hard to think of Mr. Lyle as deserving."

The Fabulous Five headed toward the school steps, but as swift as they tried to be, by the time they picked their way through the debris to the other side of the school yard, there was no trace of Mr. Lyle, the kidnappers, the Vice President, or the limousine.

"Let's look for them," said TJ. "They can't have gone far."

At that moment, two police cars entered the school yard, lights flashing, sirens wailing. The hot air balloon hovered over their cars.

Both police cars went out of control because their windshields became so splattered with paint their drivers couldn't see. Every time the drivers put their heads out of the window, the P-4 sprayed them. The two cars were going around in large circles. The two cars crashed head on.

Four police officers climbed from the two police cars. One of them was Sergeant Sweeney.

"Every time you kids are around . . ." he started to say, but broke off and quickly ran for cover.

Sam the Snitch, his hot air balloon, and the P-4 were heading his way. But this time Sergeant Sweeney was lucky.

The breeze had died down. The Perfect Portable Personality Painter had run out of paint. The hot air balloon drifted slowly down to the school yard, where just a short while ago cars and people had gone over, under, and through all the decorations that had been so carefully set up.

The hot air balloon hovered for a moment over crepe paper, wood, signs, and food, scattering them in all directions. Then slowly, silently, in the midst of the mess and right beside Sergeant Sweeney, the balloon came down to rest.

Sam popped up from the gondola. "Hi, guys," he said brightly. "Wasn't that something! At first I was scared stiff. I'm afraid of heights, you know—but after a while, it almost began to be fun."

At the sight of Sam, Sergeant Sweeney's face grew redder and redder. His mouth hung open as though he were trying to say something but was unable to get the words out. Finally he managed. "Is he part of your gang, too?"

"No way!" said the Fabulous Five in unison.

The sergeant seemed to have gotten his wind back. "We heard the Vice President was being kidnapped."

"That's just it. She's already disappeared," said TJ.

"What!" the police exclaimed.

"Yes," said TJ. "We were going to look for her when . . ."

Just then Warren Wisdom, Professor's brother, came running up. "Police!" he said. "Boy, am I glad to see you. Somebody stole my van."

"What did he look like?" asked the sergeant.

"I don't know. I didn't pay any attention," said Warren Wisdom. "I just saw this big gun."

"Did he look like a Secret Service man?" asked TJ.

Warren thought for a minute. "Gee, I don't know," he finally said. "What do Secret Service men look like?"

"I don't think he's going to be much help," said Doc.

"I don't either," said TJ.

"Let me give you my license number," said Warren Wisdom to Sergeant Sweeney, who wrote it down.

"The van is light green, and it's got a dent in the front left fender, and . . . " Warren continued.

"Never mind," Sergeant Sweeney roared. "Be off with you now. We've got to look for clues. We've got no time to waste talking to a bunch of dingledangle kids."

15 NO CLUES ARE BAD NEWS

The Fabulous Five sat glumly inside the treehouse.

"There should be something we could do to save her," said TJ.

"If there is, I can't think of it," said Doc. "I've been mulling it over and over. Whoever pulled that kidnap caper is either very smart or very lucky."

"I've been watching the television news ever since we got here," said Cookie, pointing to the screen. "Nobody can figure out where they've gone."

"The kidnappers promised to make an announcement at 4:00. It's 2:30 now," said Doc.

"I wonder if she was wearing her tooth," TJ murmured.

"TJ, I'm afraid this day's been too much for you," said Mary Jane. "Why are you worrying about teeth at a time like this?"

"Not teeth. A tooth," said TJ. "I saw it in my dad's notes. One of the last things he invented was a microscopic transmitting device. It could be implanted in a tooth. He sent the information to the Secret Service."

"But did they use it?" asked Professor.

"I don't know," said TJ. "I think so, but I'm not sure."

"Is there any way we could check?" asked Doc.

"If there is some information, it might be here," said TJ.

She pressed her palm against the secret bookcase drawer. "My father's files are here."

"Are those top secret?" asked Doc.

"Oh no, he'd never let me see those," said TJ. "This is old stuff. I can tell you about it because you're sworn to secrecy."

TJ pulled out an armful of folders and passed them around. "You look through these," she said.

"Your father may be a genius," said Doc, as she riffled through a file folder, "but he sure doesn't have a good record-keeping system. Everything here is all mixed up."

"I know," said TJ. "I offered to straighten it out for him while he was gone. But he said he'd never be able to find anything if I did."

They were down to the next-to-last folder when Professor discovered what they were looking for—a letter from the Secret Service thanking TJ's father for his tooth implant invention and saying that they planned to use it as soon as possible.

"Do you think they did?" asked Cookie.

"They might have," said TJ. "The letter is dated six months ago."

"Suppose they did implant one in her tooth. How would it work?" asked Doc.

"The microscopic transmitting device would send out a special signal that could be tracked by airborne microbeam tracking equipment," said TJ.

"Then if she is wearing it, they should be able to find her without any trouble," said Mary Jane. "It wouldn't matter if she's in a car or a house or anywhere."

"Unfortunately, it would," TJ said. "You see, if the transmitter is too powerful, it could be dangerous for the wearer. It has to be a weak device to be safe. My father thought that if the President or Vice President did get kidnapped, the Secret

Service would be able to get there right away. I don't think he figured anyone would ever be kidnapped by the Secret Service!" TJ shook her head sadly.

"So what you mean," Doc said, "is that this signal can't be tracked if she is under heavy cover."

"Right," said TJ. "In fact, it won't even work if she's on the bottom floor of a two-story building."

"How about a one-story building under heavy trees?" asked Professor.

"Maybe," said TJ. "I don't think the trees would block the signal unless the foliage was very thick."

"So if she were in a car, the microbeam would pick up the signal without any trouble," said Mary Jane.

"That's right," said TJ.

"I think some clues are emerging," Doc said. "Let's assume the Vice President is wearing a transmitter tooth. If the kidnappers were still on the road, they would have already been spotted by the microbeam scanning equipment, right?"

Everyone nodded.

"So they must already be at their hideout, right?"

They nodded again.

"I see what you're saying," said TJ. "If the kidnappers' hideout were someplace far away, they would have been caught getting there. Since they haven't been caught, they must be someplace close—close enough for them to reach before any helicopters got airborne."

Mary Jane pointed out that this hideout probably had to be at least two stories tall because the microbeam scanning equipment would track the tooth transmitter otherwise.

"Why don't we start looking for her?" said TJ.

"Before we do that," said Cookie, "I think we should ask Poindexter for some help. He's always sitting around reading murder mysteries."

TJ turned to Poindexter, who was doing just that. "How about it, Poindexter? Please give us a clue." Poindexter promptly flashed on his screen:

Anyone who's not a fool
Knows many things begin at school.

"That doesn't make much sense," said Cookie.
"Give us another clue," said Doc.
Poindexter gave them a second message:

You asked me for *a* clue.
I gave you *one*. I'll not give you two.

He picked up his book and headed off towards a corner, completely ignoring their requests for more help.

"I guess we'll have to do the best we can with what we've got," said TJ.

"Begin at school," Professor murmured. "That's where the kidnapping began."

"Maybe that's where we should begin, too," said TJ. She unrolled a map of Hillcrest. "Here's the school," she said. "So we should ride our bikes out about this far and look for a place at least two stories high."

"That's only if she's wearing the tooth," said Doc. "It's more important for us to search for the getaway car. It could be either Warren's van or the limousine. But whichever it is, it has to be hidden out of sight."

"Let's go, then," said TJ. "We'll meet back here in one hour to listen to the kidnapper's announcement. Maybe then we can pick up some more clues."

TJ was the first to arrive back at the treehouse. Much to her surprise, she saw something that looked like a sausage-shaped mummy dangling from the platform.

"What's that?" asked TJ, as soon as she magnabeamed up.

"What's that?" asked Doc and Professor who were right behind her.

"What's that?" asked Mary Jane who followed them.

"I don't know," said TJ. "I just got here myself and I haven't had a chance to find out."

She looked around.

"Poindexter?" TJ asked. Poindexter waved his hand at her absentmindedly and continued reading.

"Bartholomew?" TJ asked. At the sound of his name, Bartholomew got up and started dusting with one hand and sweeping the floor with the other.

"What's the matter with him?" asked Mary Jane. "This place is perfectly clean already."

"I don't know," said Doc. "He sure is acting strange."

"Bartholomew, I want to talk to you," said TJ.

Bartholomew dropped the dustrag and broom, quickly filled a pail with water, took a sponge, and started washing the windows.

"Bartholomew . . ." TJ began, but the robot paid no attention. He wiped off the windows with a cloth. Then he sloshed water on the walls and started washing them down.

"Stop immediately!" TJ shouted. "Or I'll discharge your batteries."

Bartholomew dropped his sponge and stood at stiff attention.

"What's this all about?" TJ demanded.

Since Bartholomew had no speaking mechanism of his own, he had to depend on Poindexter for communication. Bartholomew trundled over to Poindexter, tapped him on the shoulder, and blinked some red and green lights at him.

Poindexter nodded. Then he printed out the following message:

> An uninvited guest
> Can be a pest.
> So if one does appear,
> We do our best
> To help him rest
> As long as he is here.

"Was he a boy with slicked back hair and shiny shoes?" asked Doc.

Bartholomew nodded up and down.

"Sam the Snitch!" said TJ, Mary Jane, Doc, and Professor, all at the same time.

"What about Sam the Snitch?" asked Cookie, who had just arrived. "And what's that thing out there hanging from the platform?"

"That thing is Sam the Snitch," explained TJ. "He was probably snooping around, ignoring our 'Do Not Trespass' signs. I guess Bartholomew gave him a shot of sleep ray, dropped the net on him, and wrapped him up until we got home."

Bartholomew nodded his head proudly and clapped his hands.

"It's imperative that we dispose of the unwelcome intruder in some manner," said Professor. "The sleep ray is only temporary, and he'll be even more suspicious when he wakes up."

"I know what we can do," said TJ. "First, we have to get him down to the ground and unwrapped. And be careful. We don't want to drop him on his head."

Fortunately, Bartholomew had attached Sam by the pulley arrangement, and the Fabulous Five were able to lower him without any serious problems. Then they unwrapped the cloth covering.

"He ought to be waking up soon," TJ said. "And when he does, Doc, you've got to be here and hypnotize him as soon as he opens his eyes."

Just then Sam's eyelids began to flutter. He opened his eyes. He started to ask where he was and what was happening. But before he could get a word out, he saw a gold coin swinging in front of his eyes and heard a soothing voice urging him to sleep, sleep, sleep.

Doc's voice continued, "Sam, you were asleep. You had a dream that you wanted to visit TJ, and you started sleepwalking. We found you here in TJ's yard, sound asleep at the foot of her tree. That's very dangerous, Sam. You must never, never, never visit TJ's yard again. It's too dangerous. When I snap my fingers, you will wake up and want to go home immediately."

Doc snapped her fingers.

Sam the Snitch opened his eyes. "Where am I? Am I at TJ's house?" he asked.

"Yes, you are," said Doc. "We found you here, sound asleep."

"Oh! That's terrible," said Sam. I had this dream. I must have been sleepwalking. I want to go home. I want to go home now. I never, never, never want to come back here."

And he jumped up and ran out of the gate, shouting, "No! I never want to come back here!"

"Well," said Doc. "That takes care of Sam."

"I hope so," said TJ. "But we've got more important things to do. Has anybody found any clues at all? I looked all over the place. There just wasn't anywhere that the van or limousine could have been hidden."

"That was the same way with me," said Doc. "I didn't find one clue."

"Me, neither," said Mary Jane gloomily.

"Nor I," said Professor. "How about you, Cookie?"

"You remember that real old house at the end of the long dirt road on Oak Street?" Cookie asked. "I'd practically forgotten about it until I went past there today. The road's set way back and hidden by a row of thick hedges. I followed it to the house. The house is only one story high, but there are the thickest trees around it that I ever saw. I wanted to get closer, but there's barbed wire running all around the property."

"Was there any place to conceal a vehicle?" asked Professor.

"There was a garage or a shed or something out in back. I looked for tire marks on the dirt road, but I didn't see any. The place really looked deserted, but I think we ought to check it out some more."

"I do, too," said Mary Jane. "Let's go now."

"We can't leave yet. It's one minute to four. The kidnappers said that they would make an announcement then," Doc

109

reminded them.

"Oh, my gosh, that's right," said Mary Jane. "I almost forgot."

TJ adjusted the television set. The announcer was saying, "The kidnappers have promised that they would give out a message at four o'clock, but they did not say who they would give this message to or how they would send it. It is already past four and we have received no word from them yet."

The Fabulous Five watched the set intently. Bartholomew, who never watched anything on television but the horse races, was watching. Even Poindexter put down his book and was staring at the screen.

"Ladies and gentlemen," the announcer said excitedly, "we have just learned that there has been a message sent to the Secret Service that said the kidnappers weren't ready to discuss anything yet. When the Secret Service traced the call, they found out a recording device had been left in a phone booth just outside the Secret Service office. It was timed to call at four o'clock."

"That was very clever of them," said TJ. "I think these criminals are going to be hard to catch."

"Meanwhile," the announcer continued, "Hillcrest police have found an abandoned van stolen at gunpoint from a Hillcrest resident, Mr. Warren Wisdom. The van was discovered on the Old West Road north of Oak Street an hour ago. The whole area has been sealed off by the authorities while experts check for clues and fingerprints."

"Hey!" said Cookie. "That's near that old house I was talking about."

"Do you suppose the kidnappers are there?" asked Mary Jane.

"They might be," said TJ. "We've got to go there immediately. Let's leave one at a time."

"Where will we meet?" asked Doc.

"Behind the row of hedges—unless the cops are there," said TJ. "If they are, just act casual and come back here."

16 A SLIP OF THE LIP

TJ arrived last. "Did you see any cops?" she asked. "I didn't."

"They must all be over on the Old West Road with the van," said Professor.

"Maybe they don't even know about this house," said Doc.

"If they don't, they're sure to discover it soon," said TJ. "We've got to move fast and be extra careful."

TJ took off her glasses and twisted the lenses. Inside were powerful magnifying glasses that she used when she wanted to study things up close. No wonder her glasses looked so thick. Without those special magnifying lenses, they would be just like most other glasses. TJ got down on her hands and knees and studied the area carefully.

"I don't see any tire tracks," she said.

"Maybe they put the car somewhere else and walked up here," said Professor.

"Possible," said TJ, "but not very probable. There are no footprints except Cookie's."

TJ continued to follow the path on her hands and knees, shaking her head sadly. "It certainly doesn't look promising," she murmured.

When they got to the barbed wire, Doc and Professor found tree branches and used them to prop up the bottom strand so they could crawl underneath. Very stealthily, one by one, they slid under the barbed wire fence. The Fabulous Five were protected by the tall grass which they crawled through on their stomachs.

They surrounded the house. They looked through the windows. Dust covered the floor. If people had walked there recently, their footprints surely would have given them away. There was some old furniture in the living room which looked like mice had gotten into it and eaten out the stuffing.

"I wish we had more time to explore this place," said Professor. "It looks like it's been undisturbed for years."

"It looks awfully spooky to me," said Mary Jane. "Let's get out of here."

"We ought to look at that shed out in back first," said TJ. "Just to make sure that the limousine isn't hidden in there."

But when they got to the shed, they saw that there were rusty locks on the door. They could tell it hadn't been opened for a long, long time.

"It's starting to get dark," said Mary Jane. "I don't like this place at all."

"I hear something," said Professor.

The Fabulous Five listened. The sound of voices came closer. Footsteps crunched through the tall grass.

"Maybe it's the kidnappers," whispered Mary Jane.

"Or the police," whispered Doc.

"Never mind who it is," TJ's voice was urgent. "We don't want anybody to catch us here."

"Let's hurry," said Mary Jane. "I'm getting really scared."

It was hard to move quickly. The long grass seemed to reach out and hold their legs. The tall trees cast menacing shadows on the ground, and branches scratched at their arms. They were glad to be back at the street again.

"Well," said Cookie, "I guess there wasn't anything there after all. What'll we do now?"

"Go back to the school, I guess. Maybe there's something we overlooked," said TJ.

The school grounds looked like a tornado had struck them. The remains of the carnival were strewn around everywhere. The sun had almost set.

"It's going to be dark soon," said Mary Jane.

"So we'll have to work fast," said TJ. "Let's reconstruct the events as we remember them."

"The Vice President had just made a tour of the carnival, and she was standing here with Mr. Lyle," said Doc. "There were two Secret Service agents beside her. She was about to get into the limousine."

"Then," said Professor, "two other men, who looked like they were Secret Service agents, came from over there to the side of the car, knocked down the two original agents, grabbed the Vice President, threw her into the car, and started to drive off."

"That's when the Perfect Portable Personality Painter went into action," said Mary Jane.

"Thanks to a little help from Sam the Snitch," said Doc.

"You can see the route the car took by following the paint drippings," Cookie said, adding, "I wonder why that paint dripped so much. I thought it was supposed to be fast drying."

"You can worry about that later," snapped TJ impatiently. "We're concerned with something much more important now."

Cookie sighed. It was hard to put up with TJ when she was impatient.

The Fabulous Five walked through the wreckage, tracing paint drippings.

"They drove off before anyone could stop them," said Professor. "The driver must have been part of their gang."

"I wonder what Mr. Lyle's going to do about next year's carnival," said Cookie. "I'll bet nobody's going to want to be the guest of honor after this."

"Cookie!" shouted TJ. "I told you not to worry about dumb stuff. Who cares about what Mr. Lyle is going to . . .Wait a minute!"

TJ snapped her fingers. She practically jumped up and down with excitement. "That's it! MR. LYLE!!"

"You don't mean he's one of the kidnappers," exclaimed Mary Jane. "I just can't believe that!"

"Of course he's not, Mary Jane," said TJ. "What I'm wondering is—where is Mr. Lyle?"

"He's missing," said Doc thoughtfully. "And he usually likes to be right in the middle of things."

"Maybe he's so mortified about what occurred at the carnival that he's too embarrassed to be seen," suggested Professor.

"I'd expect him to be out leading the chase to find those kidnappers. To uphold the honor of Hillcrest Junior High School or something," said Doc.

Mary Jane added, "I'd expect him to be out protecting his car. You know how much he loves that Rolls Royce."

"In all the confusion about the Vice President's being kidnapped, nobody's given a thought to Mr. Lyle," said TJ.

"Do you think they kidnapped him as well?" asked Cookie.

"It wouldn't surprise me at all," said TJ. "They tried to earlier when they wanted his car."

"Does anybody remember seeing Mr. Lyle after he got away from the kidnapper?" asked Doc. "We ought to concentrate because it's important."

They all thought for a moment, but no one was able to remember anything.

"There has to be a solution here somewhere," murmured TJ. "Both of the kidnappers came from that direction, near the storage shed."

"The storage shed! That's it!" It was Doc who said it, but the thought hit all of them at the same time.

The storage shed was big enough to hide the limousine.

The Fabulous Five started to rush over.

"Wait," whispered TJ. "We've got to be more careful. Suppose they've got somebody guarding it."

They approached silently and cautiously. No one was in sight.

"Do you suppose it's been sound-scanned?" asked Mary Jane.

"I'll test it," TJ said. She picked up a large stone and threw it so it landed right in front of the door.

"If it's sound-scanned," said TJ, "someone will be out here pretty fast."

It was only five minutes of anxious waiting, but it seemed like an hour until TJ said, "It's all right. But we'd still better be careful. Before we go any further, let me check the ground for footprints."

TJ tiptoed to the shed and knelt down. As she had done before, she took off her glasses and twisted out the special magnifying lens. By now, it was so dark she could hardly see. She bent very close to the ground.

"Someone has come out of here recently," she said. "But whoever it was, covered up the footprints with his hand."

"Where did he go?" asked Cookie.

"As far as there," said TJ, pointing to the grass nearby. "I can't trace him after that."

"At least we know someone was here recently and tried to hide that fact," said Doc.

"Let's examine the storage shed now," said TJ.

The door to the storage shed was tightly locked with a padlock and chain. There were no windows to look through. But there was a small air vent close to the roof.

"Doc, we're the tallest," Professor said. "If you get up on my shoulders, you might be able to look through that air vent."

Doc stretched as far as she could, but she could barely see inside."

"It's just too dark to see anything," she told them.

"Let me give the padlock a try," said TJ. "I've been reading about locks, and I'd like to see if I've learned anything."

115

The others waited while she turned the lock back and forth.

"That's it!" she said on the third try. She opened the lock. They lifted off the chain and cautiously opened the door.

"We've got to be quiet about this," warned TJ.

The Fabulous Five opened the door as quietly as they could, but the hinges were rusty and let out an awful squeak.

"I think I can see it," said TJ, as she stuck her head around the corner of the door. "Yes. It's here! The limousine is here."

"We better get out of here," said Mary Jane. "If we get caught, we're in big trouble."

"Let's go down the block," said Doc. "We can talk better there."

"The kidnappers must be in the school," said Professor.

"Yes. That's how they were able to get away so quickly," TJ said. "They didn't have to get away at all. In all that confusion, they just slipped around to the back. No wonder the helicopters couldn't find them."

"The school is two stories tall," said Doc. "If they're on the first floor, the microbeam scanning equipment wouldn't pick up the signal from the Vice President's tooth."

"If she's wearing it," said Mary Jane.

"We better scout around," said TJ. "Be very quiet."

By now, the lights in the school yard were on. In order not to be seen, the Fabulous Five ran swiftly into the shadows and crouched against the building as close as they could.

"There seems to be a light on in Mr. Lyle's office," whispered Mary Jane.

They crept noiselessly to the lighted window. Although the shades had been drawn, they weren't quite long enough to reach the windowsill.

By standing on his toes, Professor could just manage to see into Mr. Lyle's office. The Vice President was there. Her hands were tied behind the back of her chair, and a gag was tied over her mouth.

Facing her in another chair and bound exactly the same

116

way was Mr. Lyle. Professor could see five men guarding them, but he could tell at a glance that the two prisoners were tied so tightly that they couldn't have gotten away, even if there were no guards.

In sign language, Professor told the others what he had just seen. Suddenly, they heard footsteps.

"Quick, around the corner," whispered TJ.

They ran around the corner and lay flat on the ground where a large shrub cut off most of the light.

All except Cookie. He tripped and didn't make it in time.

Cookie scrunched up close to the wall. From where the others lay, they could see a man running with a pistol in his hand. A second man was close behind him."

"See anybody?"

"No. No one at all. It must have been your imagination."

"I could have sworn I heard voices out here," insisted the second man.

"You're as shaky as a palm tree in a hurricane. Nothing's going to go wrong. They haven't found us yet. We're safe, I tell you," the man with the pistol said.

"I guess you're right. I still think someone should stand guard outside."

"I told you a hundred times already. It might make someone suspicious. There's never a guard out here. We don't want to do anything out of the ordinary."

He put his pistol in his pocket. "Come on, let's go inside."

"All right," his partner agreed reluctantly.

They started back to the school.

Just then Cookie sneezed.

"Who's that?" asked the kidnapper.

He pointed his gun right at the spot where Cookie was hiding. "Whoever's there, come out here in the light or I'll shoot!"

His partner grabbed Cookie by the shirt as he stepped forward. "Who are you, kid? And what are you doing here this time of night?"

"I'm C-C-Cookie C-C-Cook," said Cookie. "Why-why-why are you pointing that g-g-gun at m-m-me?"

"I'll ask the questions, kid. If you give the right answers, the gun won't go off. But if you give the wrong ones. . ."

The man didn't finish the sentence. He didn't have to.

"I-I-I'll tell you whatever you want t-t-to know," said Cookie.

"What are you doing here?"

"I had a b-b-booth today at the carnival, and it got wrecked. I left some of my stuff inside, and I came back to get it."

"Why didn't you get it earlier?"

"I w-w-wanted to w-w-watch the news on television. I w-w-wanted to see if my picture was on."

Cookie's friends listened intently to this conversation.

Doc pressed on her transmitium-coated nail, "Cookie sure is thinking fast."

Professor answered the same way, "The kidnappers seem to believe him."

"Why'd you come back now?" the kidnapper asked Cookie.

"My m-m-mom made me. She said my stuff might get ripped off if I left it overnight."

"What do you think?" asked the man who had been doing all the questioning.

"He sounds like he's telling the truth to me," said the other. "But we can't take a chance and let him go. He might tell somebody something about what's going on here."

"Oh, I won't tell anybody about anything," said Cookie. "I promise. I won't tell anybody about who you've got tied up. . . in. . . oh-oh!"

But it was too late.

One man put his hand over Cookie's mouth, so he couldn't make a sound. The other put his gun close to Cookie's head and said, "Okay, kid, let's go."

He grabbed Cookie by the arm. The two men dragged Cookie inside the school building.

17 THE CAPER'S COMPLETE

"**T**his is awful," muttered Professor. "I hope they won't do him bodily harm."

"Me, too," said Mary Jane. "Kidnapping the Vice President was bad enough. But now that they've got Cookie, too, it's horrible."

"We'll have to get them," said Doc. "We've just got to rescue Cookie."

"If we don't do something fast, they're liable to shoot him," said Professor.

"Oh, I hope not," said Mary Jane. "I just hate blood. I just hate guns. I wish they'd invent guns that don't make people bleed."

"But they do," said Doc. "At least TJ's dad did. We've got the sleepgun back at the treehouse."

"Of course!" exclaimed TJ. "Why didn't I think of that? I'll run back and get it right now."

"I have to hurry," TJ thought, her heart pounding as she ran. "They need me back there."

When she got to the treehouse, she magnabeamed up and

started looking for the sleepgun, pushing aside the papers that Bartholomew had stacked so neatly.

"Bartholomew," she shouted, "where's the sleepgun?"

The small robot scurried over and held up his hand. The sleepgun was in it. The light at the top of his pointed hat was blinking on and off.

"You're recharging it? Now? But what'll I do?"

Poindexter, who had put his book down as soon as TJ entered, trundled over and flashed the message: "Call your father."

"Call Daddy? Now? But I've got to get back. And he said not to call unless it was a super emergency."

Poindexter's screen went dark. Then the same message: "Call your father" appeared, followed by the word *immediately*.

TJ went to the ultra long distance laserphone and touched three numbers, waited, and then touched eight more. She could hear a buzzing at the other end.

"Maybe he's not there," she said to Bartholomew and Poindexter. "It's buzzed eleven times already."

On the twelfth buzz, she heard a familiar voice say, "Hello?"

"Oh, Daddy, is that you? It's me, TJ."

"What's the matter? Is anything wrong?"

"Some fake Secret Service men have kidnapped the Vice President, Daddy. And Cookie, too, They're tied up in the school. And they might be killed. We're going to rescue them."

"Who's going to do it?"

"Me and Doc and Mary Jane and Professor."

"Get the police, TJ. They'll help."

"They won't, Daddy. They won't believe us. They haven't believed anything we've said so far."

There was a pause.

"Use the sleepgun, TJ."

"I wanted to. But Bartholomew's recharging it."

"All the better. Take him. And Poindexter, too. They'll help."

"I will."

120

"And be careful, TJ. Be careful because I love you."

"I love you, too, Daddy."

"Good luck, TJ. I know you can do it. Goodbye."

TJ hung up the laserphone. "I sure wish he was here," she whispered. Then she turned to Poindexter and Bartholomew.

"You heard what he said. We've got to hurry. We've got to do it right. They're depending on us back there."

"I wonder where she could be?" asked Doc. "She sure is slow."

"I think she's coming now," said Professor.

But to their surprise she wasn't alone.

"What are they doing here?" Mary Jane asked.

"Bartholomew is recharging the sleepgun by running it off his own circuits. We can't use it unless he's here," TJ explained. "And when I called my father, he said to bring them both."

Bartholomew's hat blinked three times.

"I'm not sure this is a good idea." Mary Jane tapped the message so that neither Bartholomew or Poindexter would hear.

"Well, I am," TJ tapped back. "My father never makes mistakes about important things."

"What'll Poindexter do?" asked Doc.

Poindexter turned to them with the following message:

All of life's a mystery.
And action is a part of it.
Why stay home and merely read
When you can be the heart of it?

"I sure hope he rescues better than he writes poetry," muttered Professor.

Poindexter's screen went blank. He turned abruptly away from them.

"Now look what you've done," said TJ.

"I apologize, Poindexter," said Professor. "My utterance was tactless and tasteless."

"Besides," said TJ, "this is no time for literary criticism

121

or hurt feelings."

Poindexter turned around with another message: "Apology accepted."

"That's good," said TJ. "Let's not waste any more time. We've got to get into that building."

"There may be an unlocked window on the second floor," said Doc.

"I'll check," said TJ.

Nimbly climbing a nearby tree, she went hand over hand to the tip of an outer limb, then swung to the narrow ledge beneath the window and tried to open it.

It was unlocked.

TJ opened it wide enough to get through, and then she climbed back down the tree to consult with the others.

"We can't attack without the sleepgun," TJ said, "and we can't have the sleepgun without Bartholomew. So I'll go up through the window, sneak down through the halls, and open the side door. Then we'll all go in and rescue them."

TJ climbed the tree one more time and crept cautiously into the dark hall, careful to make no sound that might reveal her presence. She knew that if she did, she'd be sitting right there beside Cookie.

She opened the side door for the others, and they went down the hall to Mr. Lyle's office. They could see Cookie, bound and gagged like the others.

Poindexter's message board lit up with the following words:

Raise a ruckus.
Make a fuss.
If you do that,
They'll come to us.

And without waiting for any comments on his suggestion, he bumped into Bartholomew, making an awful clang as the two metal bodies hit.

"I know there's someone out there now," said one of the kidnappers, running to the door to investigate.

As soon as he opened the door, Bartholomew zapped him with the sleepgun.

Crouching behind Bartholomew, TJ guided his hand as he held the sleepgun. The other four kidnappers were so taken by surprise that they didn't even reach for their guns. And before they knew what had happened, they were on the floor, fast asleep.

TJ, Doc, Mary Jane, and Professor quickly untied the Vice President, Cookie, and Mr. Lyle and tied up the kidnappers.

"What happened?" asked the Vice President.

"We've rescued you. You're safe now," TJ told her.

"What a relief," she said. "This has been a terrible experience. You're very brave."

"Of course they're brave!" Mr. Lyle spoke up. "At least, the human ones are. I don't know about those other two."

Then he turned and whispered to TJ so that the Vice President couldn't hear, "What are those things?"

"They're not things, they're robots. They're Bartholomew and Poindexter," said TJ indignantly. "They're . . . they're . . . they're practically part of my family."

"I don't care what they are," said Mr. Lyle. "Just as long as you don't enroll them in Hillcrest Junior High School."

And he headed for the telephone to call the police.

It seemed that the sirens sounded outside just as soon as Mr. Lyle hung up the telephone.

"We better have a plan for leaving the building," said TJ.

"A plan!" exclaimed Mr. Lyle. "What do we need a plan for? All we have to do is simply walk out the door."

"Hands up! Hands up!" The voice thundered over a loudspeaker. "We've got you surrounded."

"We're coming," they shouted.

The police evidently had not heard them. "Come out with your hands up," repeated the voice. "If you're not out by the count of ten we'll shoot. One. . . two. . . three. . . "

"This is dangerous," said Mr. Lyle. "I told them over the telephone that we were already out of danger."

123

"Four. . . five. . . six. . . "

"This is Mr. Lyle," the principal shouted to the police. "WE ARE ALL RIGHT!! THE VICE PRESIDENT IS SAFE!!"

"Seven. . . eight. . . nine. . . "

"Oh dear," murmured Ms. Blanchard. "It would be dreadful to be rescued from your enemies only to be shot by your friends."

"Maybe we should. . . " TJ began.

"It's too late to do anything now," Mr. Lyle snapped. "Why didn't you think of something earlier?"

They rushed out of the school with their hands raised high.

"Hold your fire," shouted Sergeant Sweeney to his officers.

"Yes! Yes!" shouted Mr. Lyle. "Whatever else you do, hold your fire!"

18 WAIT TILL NEXT YEAR

The whole place was lit up with huge searchlights. Ms. Blanchard, Mr. Lyle, and the Fabulous Five were so blinded, they could hardly see the crowd that had gathered in the school yard.

"It's the Vice President!" shouted someone from the crowd as soon as the group appeared. "She's safe! She's safe!" All the people broke into applause.

"Stand back! Stand back!" the police commanded, but no one paid much attention. There were shutters clicking and strobes flashing all over the place.

The Vice President waved to the crowd. A microphone was pushed at her.

"Please say something to the nation," a reporter urged.

The Vice President smiled and said, "I'm safe. I'm well. The kidnappers are inside, tied up, and I'm sure the police and Secret Service will deal with them as necessary."

The crowd broke into a loud cheer. She held up her hand for silence.

"This has been a long ordeal for me, as you can imagine, and I am tired. However, before I go, I want to call your attention to these five young people here. Without them, I . . . we. . . would never have been rescued as soon as we were. I'd like to introduce them to you."

She waved her hand at the Fabulous Five, motioning them to come forward. "Please say your names into the microphone and look right into that camera. I want the whole world to know you brave and wonderful young people."

As each of the Fabulous Five gave his or her name, the crowd broke into wild applause. The cheering could be heard for a mile.

One person, however, stood in the background. He fidgeted first on one foot and then on the other. No one was paying any attention to him at all. Finally, he couldn't stand it any longer. He came forward.

"I'm Mr. Lyle, the principal of Hillcrest Junior High. The kidnappers got me just after they got the Vice President and made me open up the school so they could use it as a hideout. I've been tied up, too," he said into the microphone, but nobody seemed to be listening to him. Everybody was cheering the Vice President and the Fabulous Five.

The noise was tremendous. The only thing louder was the sound of a giant aerodisc approaching overhead.

"It's going to land!" said Mr. Lyle. "We've got to clear everybody out of here."

But Sergeant Sweeney was a step ahead of him. He grabbed a loudspeaker and shouted to the crowd, "Give it room to land, everybody. Stand back, so nobody will get hurt."

Because the ground was so littered with the debris from the carnival, the aerodisc was unable to land. Instead it hovered, motionless, soundless, about three feet above the ground. The crowd pressed closer to it.

By then, the police had reinforcements, and they were able to get the crowd under control. A ramp bearing the Vice Presidential seal emerged. The police stood ready to escort the Vice President to it.

"Wait a moment, please," Ms. Blanchard told the police.

She turned to the Fabulous Five. "I very much appreciate your bravery and concern," the Vice President said. "Is there any way that I can thank you?"

The Fabulous Five looked at one another. No one said a word.

Finally TJ spoke. "There is one thing, ma'am," she said. "The carnival is scheduled to run another day."

The Vice President looked around. "I doubt that. It seems in pretty bad shape."

"Oh, don't worry about that, Ms. Blanchard," interrupted Mr. Lyle who came rushing up. "We'll fix it up. Or hold it next week. Or something."

The Vice President smiled briefly. "Thank you, Mr. Lyle. I'm sure you'll think of something." She turned back to TJ. "You were saying?"

"You see, Ms. Vice President," TJ continued. "There was this machine we invented—the Perfect Portable Personality Painter—and we couldn't get it in this year's carnival."

"A small misunderstanding, ma'am, a very small misunderstanding," said Mr. Lyle.

The Vice President merely nodded her head at Mr. Lyle. "Please continue," she said to TJ.

"And if the carnival runs another day, I wondered if it would be all right if we could have a booth for the Perfect Portable Personality Painter then," TJ said.

"Of course she can!" shouted Mr. Lyle. "Anything at all. I'll build the booth myself. Don't worry about a thing, kids. Mr. Lyle will take care of everything."

The Vice President took a deep breath. "Thank you, again, Mr. Lyle. We know you'll take care of everything." Ms. Blanchard turned to TJ. "This place is so battered that it hardly seems likely that it can be rebuilt in time for another carnival day tomorrow. However, I'm sure Mr. Lyle will be happy to include you in any future carnivals this school might have."

"Certainly, Ms. Blanchard, certainly," said Mr. Lyle, his voice dripping with sincerity.

"Good," said the Vice President, "I'm glad that's settled." She shook hands with Mr. Lyle. "I must be heading back to Washington." She shook hands with each of the Fabulous Five. "I'd like all of you to visit me in Washington. You can bring your machine along with you and demonstrate it there."

Everyone cheered except Mr. Lyle, who seemed to be muttering a small prayer.

Vice President Blanchard waved to the crowd once more as she climbed the ramp to the aerodisc. The crowd cheered as it took off.

And then, pretty soon, everybody started to go home.

Except the Fabulous Five.

They looked around them.

"All our equipment is somewhere in that mess," said TJ.

"We left NOSE and EARS in the booth before the kidnapping started," said Doc. "They should still be there."

"Let's see," said TJ. "Poindexter and Bartholomew, you wait here."

The Fabulous Five made their way through the wreckage. Fortunately, their booth had been so far out of the main part of the carnival that it had been spared from the afternoon's rampage. NOSE and EARS were right where the Fabulous Five had left them.

"What a relief," said TJ, "but we still have to find the P-4."

"The last time I saw it," said Cookie, "it was in Sam's hot air balloon."

"And that landed on the steps," said Mary Jane.

With TJ carefully carrying NOSE and EARS, the Fabulous Five cautiously threaded their way back. The hot air balloon had been pushed into a dark corner at the top of the steps.

As the Fabulous Five approached, Doc noticed something moving under the crumpled folds of the balloon.

"Wait," she cautioned.

There were more movements. Whatever it was, it was emerging.

128

It was Bartholomew, carrying the P-4 in his arms.

The gnome-sized robot staggered under the load. Professor rushed forward and grabbed the P-4 just as Bartholomew fell to the ground and tumbled, head over heels, down the school steps.

"Is he. . . is he all right?" asked Cookie.

"Let me see," said Mary Jane.

She removed Bartholomew's tall pointed hat and ran her fingers over the place where she had inserted the solarcircuit. Then she placed her ear against his chest.

"He'll be fine," Mary Jane announced. "It's been too much excitement for him, I guess. All he needs is some sunshine for a solarcircuit recharge."

She picked up Bartholomew and cradled him in her arms. He was dirty from lying on the ground.

"I'll carry him," Doc offered.

"No," said Mary Jane. "I don't mind."

"Well," said TJ, "it's getting late. Let's get Poindexter and go home."

"I'm starving," said Cookie. "Hard work always makes me hungry."

The Fabulous Five looked around once more.

"I guess this is the end of the carnival kidnap caper," said Professor.

"Yes, but wait until next year," said TJ, as the Fabulous Five left the school yard. "I've got some really great ideas."

DATE DUE			

FIC
DOD

Dodson, Fitzhugh.

The carnival kidnap caper.